SIS BOOM BAA·A·A·A·A!

The Adventures of Princess Lil' Cap and Sir Hud the Brave

Written by Cappy McGarr & Chandler Dean

Illustrated by Bill DeOre

This Book Belongs To:

_____

A SAVIO REPUBLIC BOOK
ISBN: 978-1-63758-986-1

Sis Boom Baa!:
The Adventures of Princess Lil' Cap and Sir Hud the Brave
© 2024 by Cappy McGarr and Chandler Dean
All Rights Reserved

Designed by Pixel Mouse House
Illustrated by Bill DeOre

posthillpress.com
New York • Nashville
Published in the United States of America
Printed in Canada

Dedicated to Annette Cap and Hudson,
the greatest grandchildren in the universe.

(Tied with all the grandchildren reading this book)

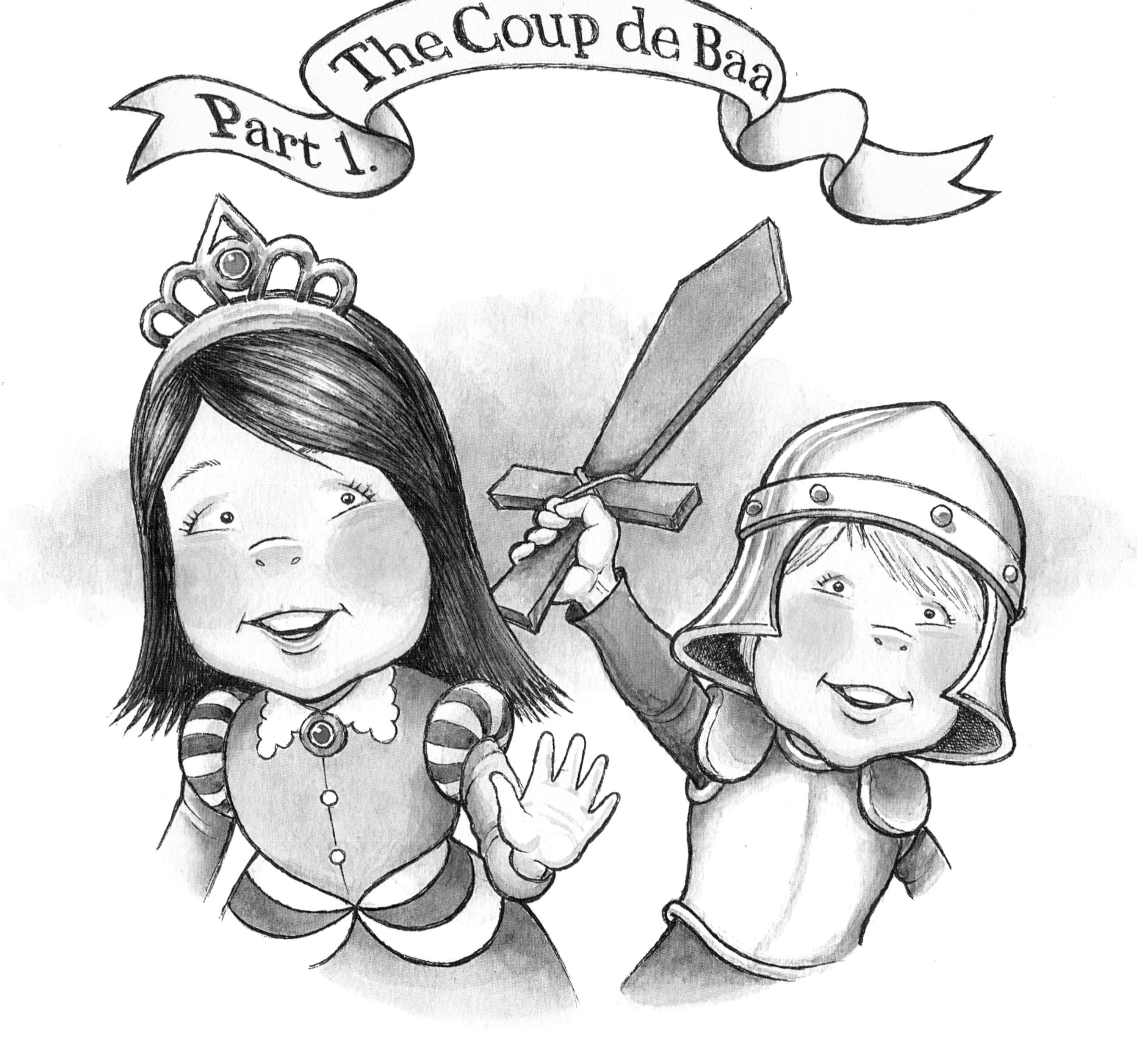
Part 1.
The Coup de Baa

This is the tale of a kingdom once saved
By Princess Lil' Cap and Sir Hud the Brave.

They lived in a castle beyond mighty ramparts;
They played and they sang and made gooseberry tarts.

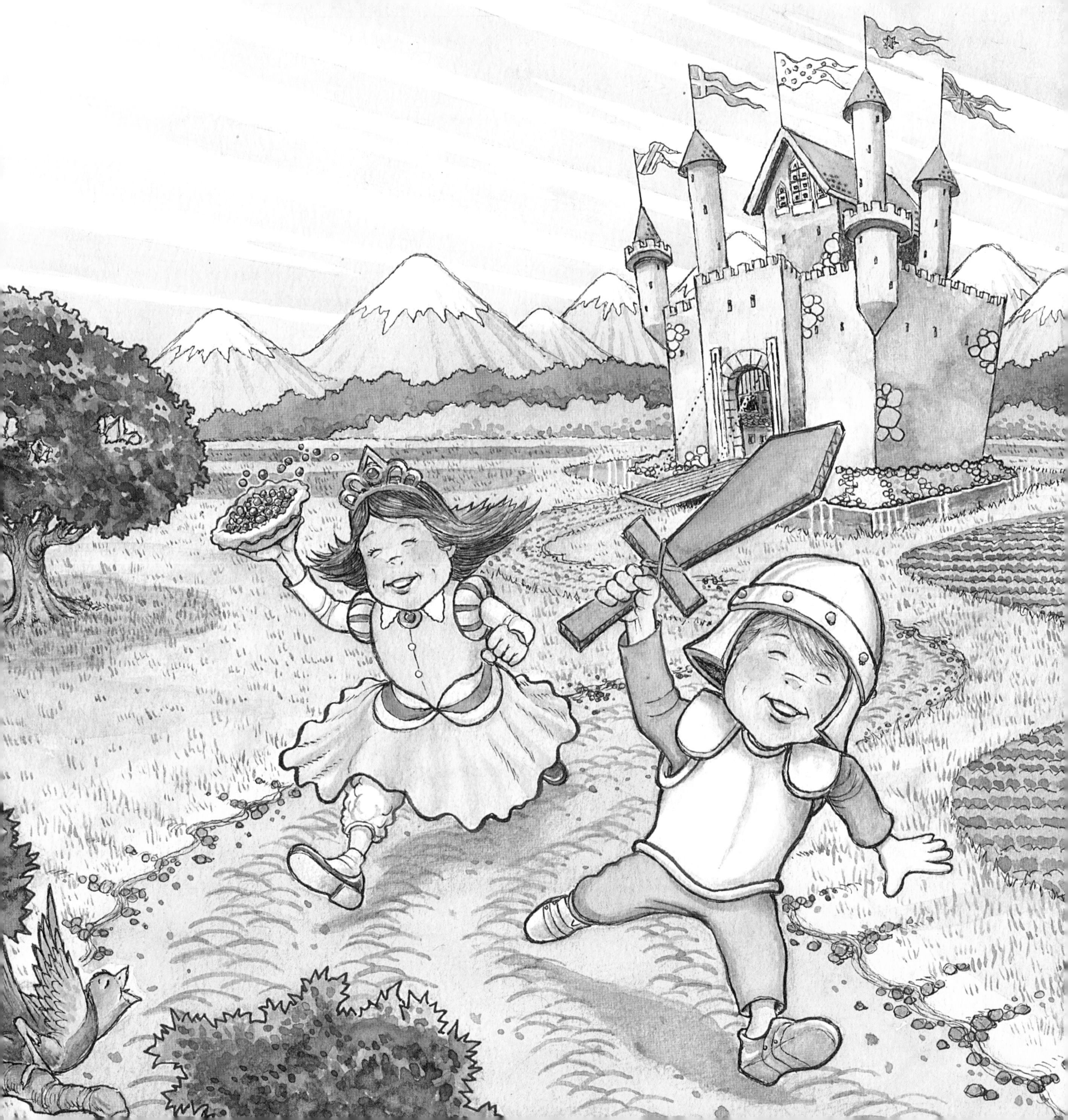

The princess read mountains of books in her suite,
But she couldn't always quite think on her feet.

Sir Hud had a good heart, was honest and true,
But he feared his own shadow and ladybugs, too!

One more royal roommate lived up in this fort;
Her name was Lambantha or just "Lam" for short.

Lam was this fair kingdom's oddest of sheep.
She never would play. She barely would peep.

But even through all of that sadness and stress,
Lil' Cap and Sir Hud both loved Lam no less.

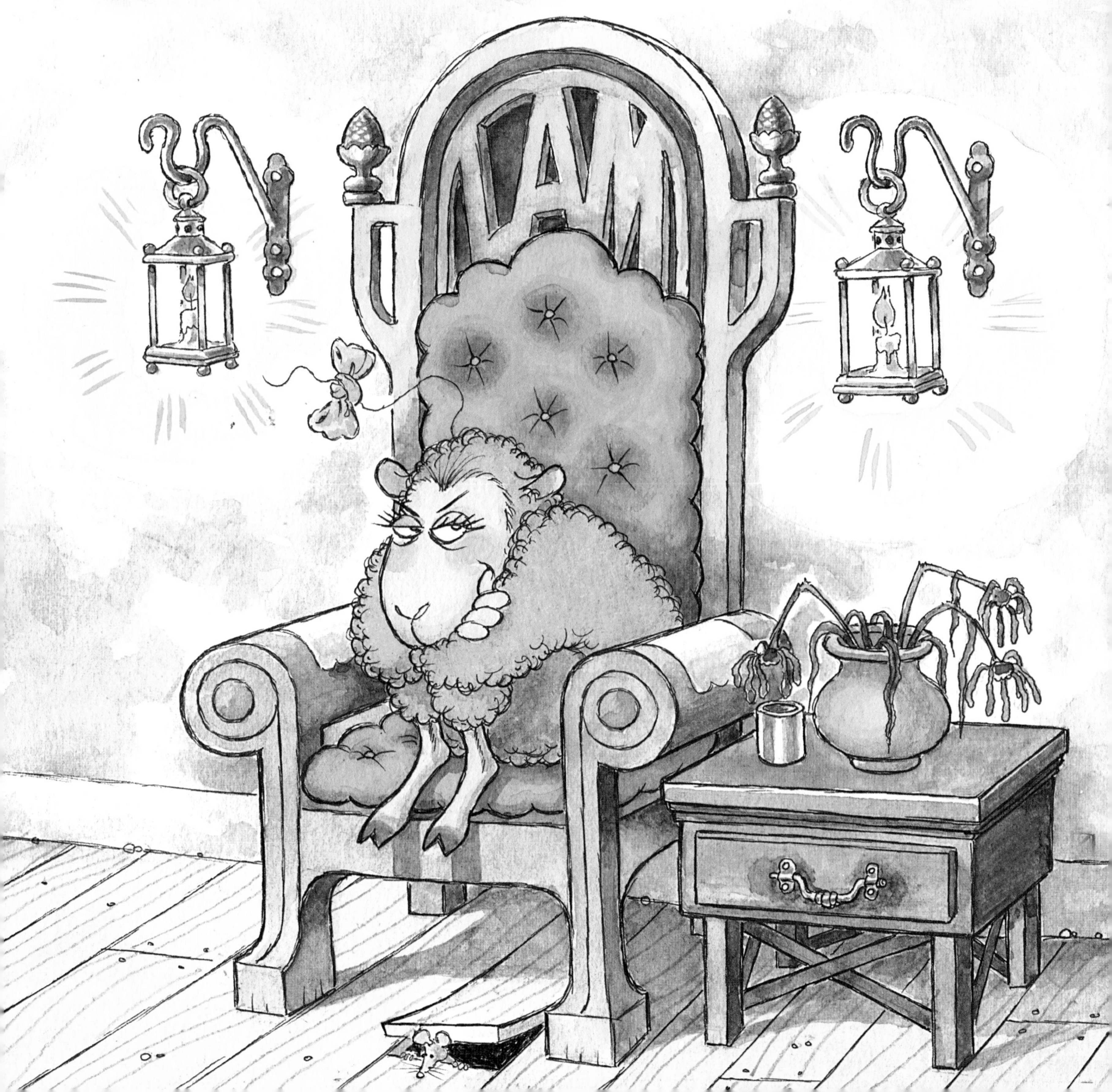

One night, as Sir Hud was lying awake,
He heard a loud thud that made his bed quake.

He followed the sound to Lil' Cap's quarters,
Where Lam had tied up the princess in short order!

"You've never considered me as your true kin,
'Cause I'm just a sheep, and y'all are human!"

Then Lam snatched Sir Hud and Lil' Cap with abandon,
And stuffed them both in the royal cannon!

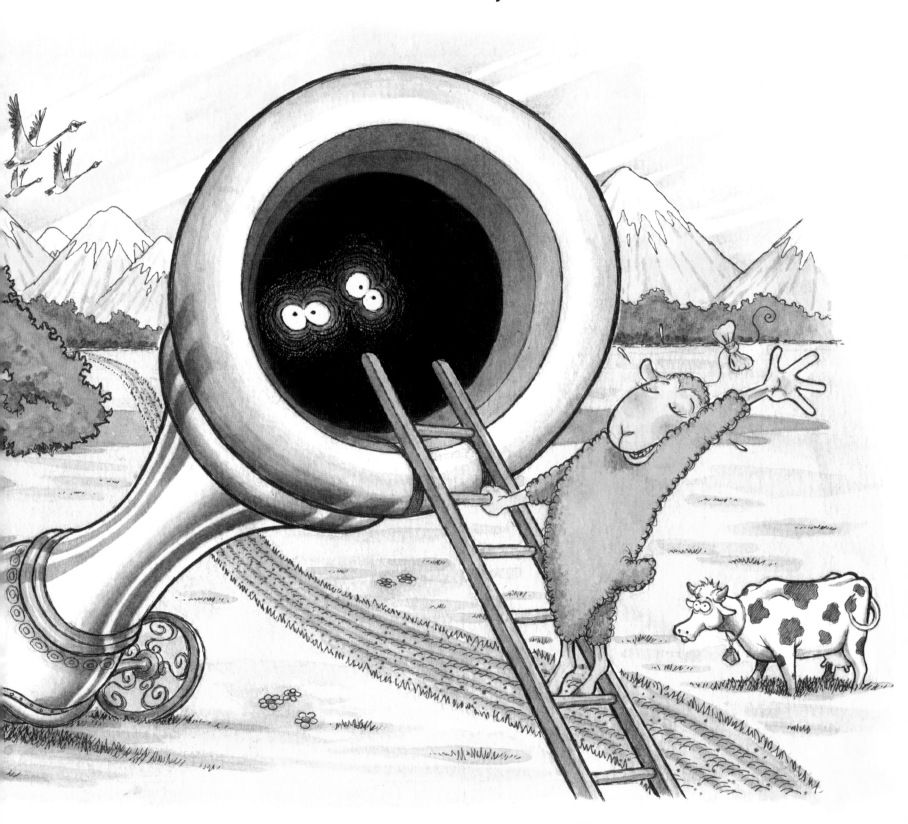

"I'll tell you this, Hud. In fact, I will shout it: There is mutton you two can do about it!"

KABOOM! And KABLAM! Hud and Cap were then fired.
No notice or paperwork even required!

They both hit the ground; Lil' Cap sprang to her feet.
"We've got to get back! We can't take this defeat!"

"I don't know," said Sir Hud. "I fear and I doubt...
There's so many hurdles. There's no easy route."

Lil' Cap was insistent: "We'll do this, you'll see!
How bad could these obstacles possibly be?"

"Real bad," worried Hud. "There's snakes, rats, and voles!
Dragons, and werewolves, and yetis, and trolls!"

Said Cap: "We'll explore deserts, forests, and caves!
And aren't you supposed to be Sir Hud the Brave?!"

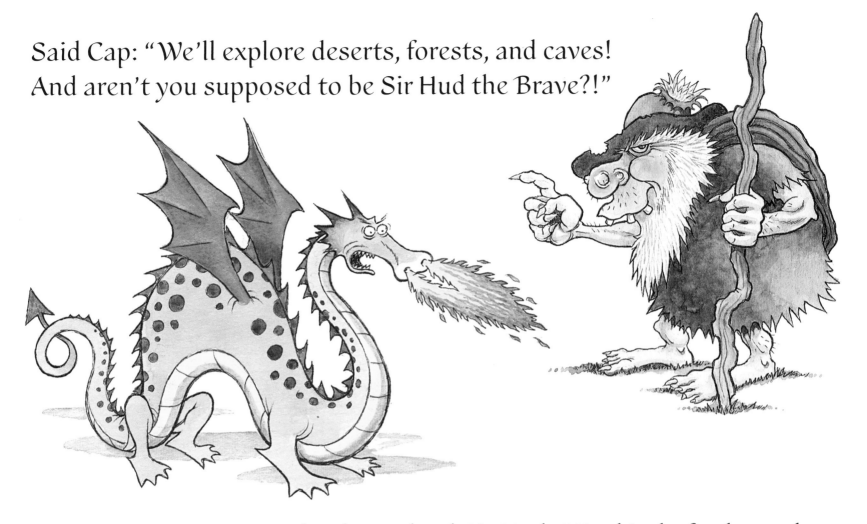

"Uh-oh," gulped Sir Hud. "I'm kind of ashamed.
'The Brave' is no title. It's just a nickname."

The princess just smiled. "Of this, I'll assure thee:
You'll learn to be brave by the end of this journey."

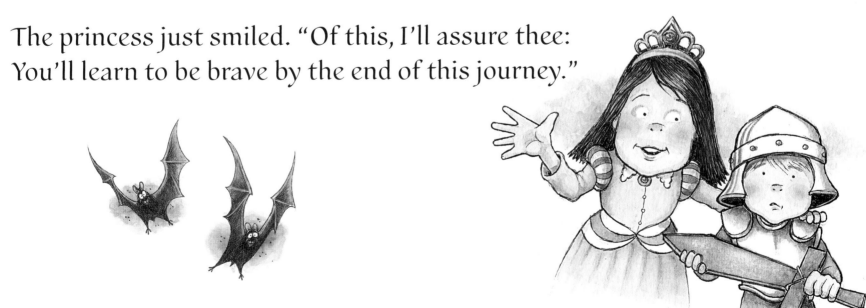

And so they took off on a long winding path,
For 8.2 miles (Lil' Cap did the math).

But then before long, Hud gasped: "I see somethin'!"
Alongside the road was a sword in a pumpkin!

Sneaking up to the squash, Lil' Cap hushed her tone:
"Have you not read of the sword in the stone?"

Hud sure enough hadn't. "Not a chance! I can't read.
Movies and TV are more of my speed."

"Try pulling that sword. If you're brave and you're true,
That powerful dagger will belong to you!"

He pulled and he tugged—he huffed and he puffed.
The sword wouldn't move! Was he not brave enough?

Hud plopped on the ground and pouted a bit.
Lil' Cap begged of him: "Please Hud, you can't quit!

"Believe you can win. Be self-confident.
That's half of the battle—it's fifty percent!"

Then he reached for the sword with great courage and nerve,
And yanked with the strength that the mission deserved!

As smooth as could be, the sword came unstuck.
Hud held it up proudly. What power! What pluck!

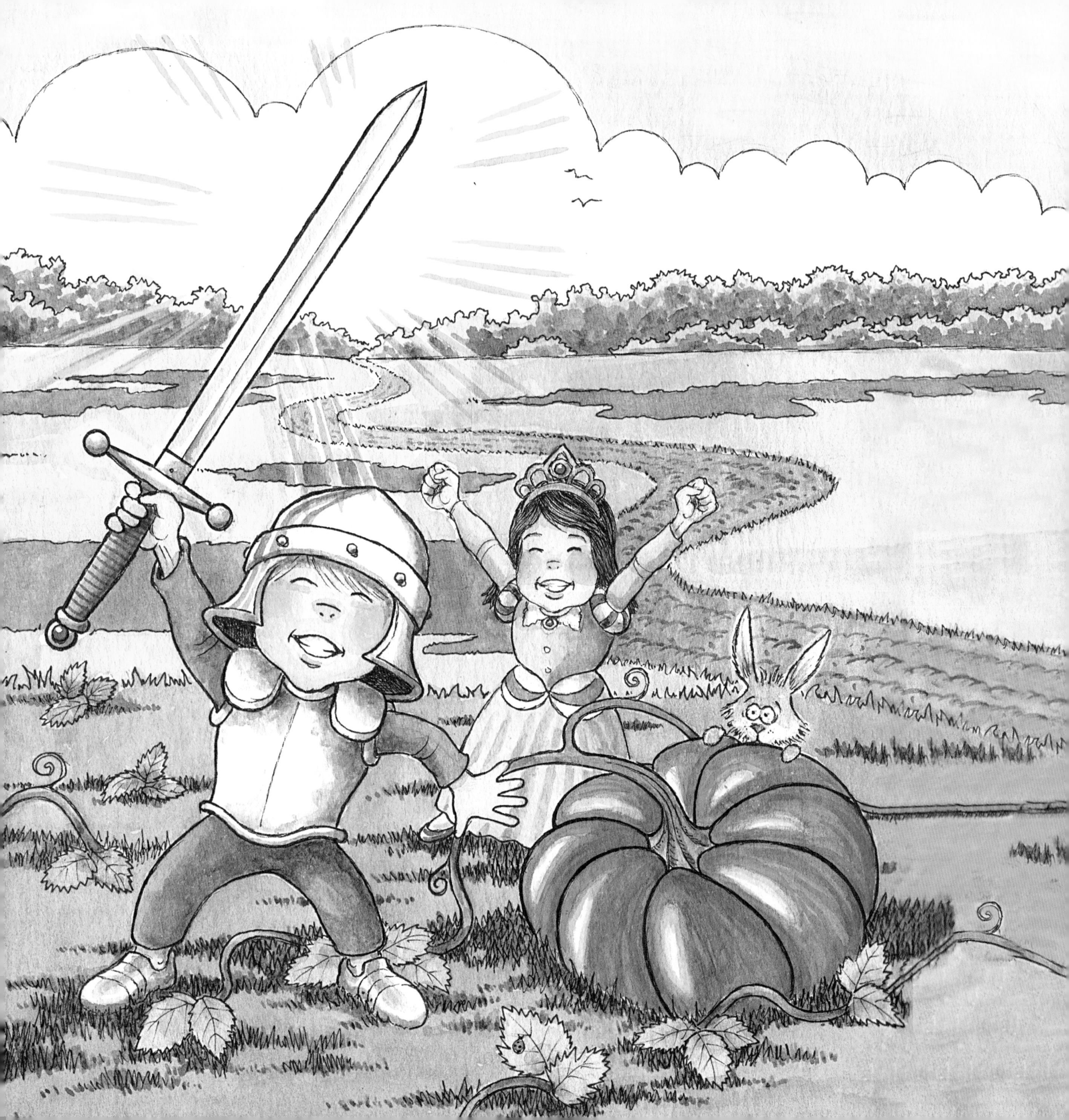

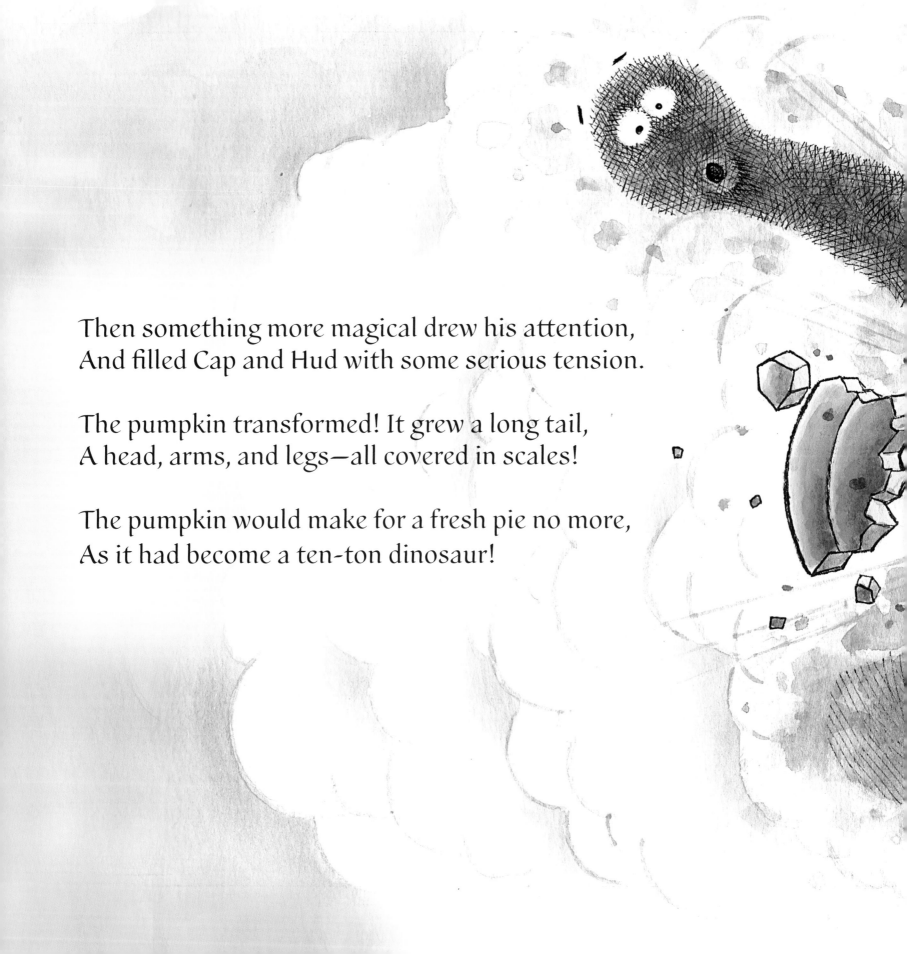

Then something more magical drew his attention,
And filled Cap and Hud with some serious tension.

The pumpkin transformed! It grew a long tail,
A head, arms, and legs—all covered in scales!

The pumpkin would make for a fresh pie no more,
As it had become a ten-ton dinosaur!

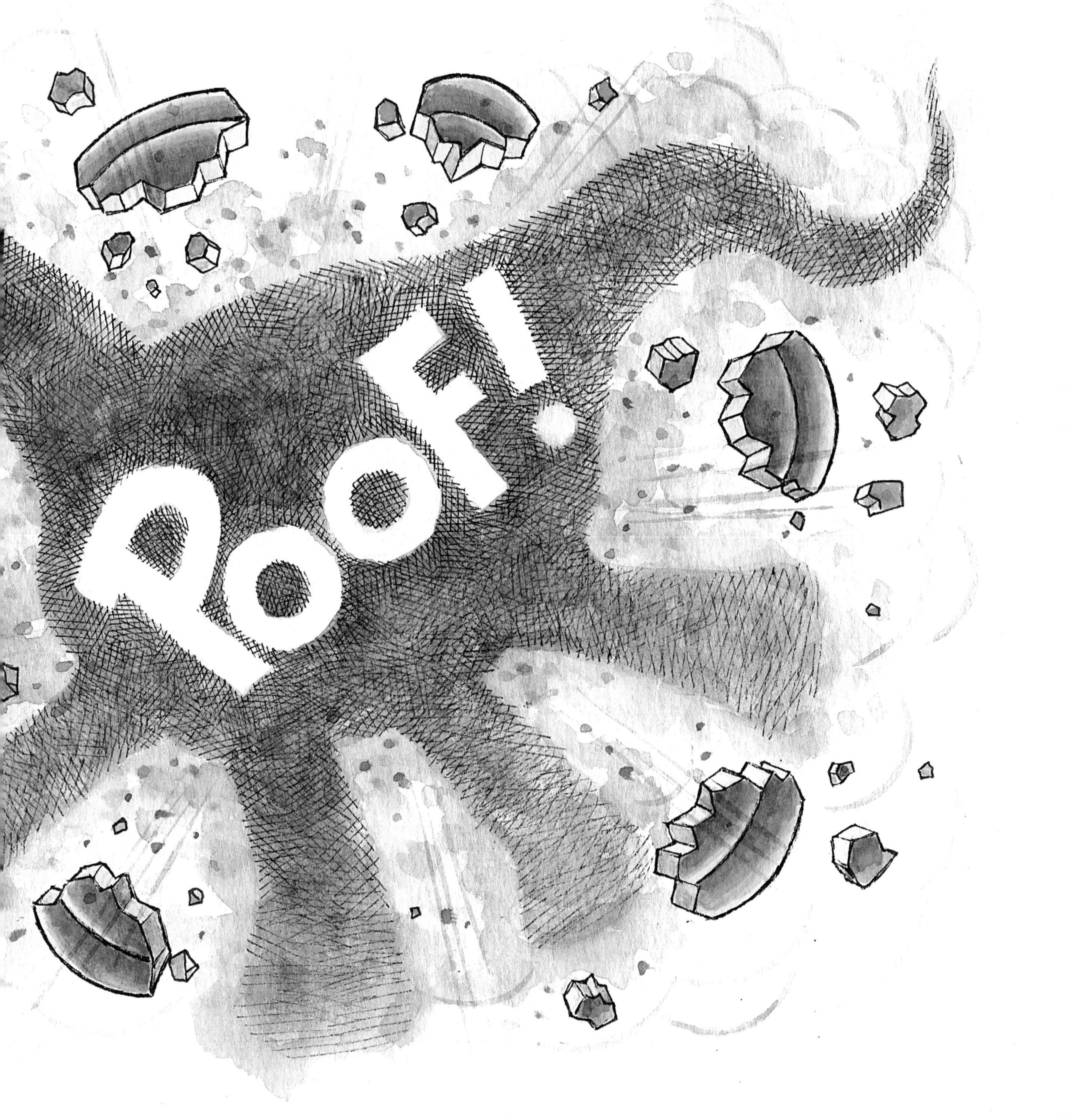
POOF!

Hud leapt to his feet and readied his blade.
"This must be a test! He's got to be slayed!"

But as he approached, the beast shed a tear,
And begged Hud to stop. "Please, sir, have no fear!

"My name's Foofasaurus, or Foofy for short—
The last sort of creature that you'd need to thwart.

"I've been in a spell—friends, don't be alarmed!
I'm big, but I'm gentle. I mean you no harm."

"We trust you," said Hud. "You seem sweet and kind.
You're just the companion we've needed to find!

"We need someone strong to help us get back.
And you could protect us if we get attacked!"

Foofy sighed. "Well, I owe you for un-hexing me.
I'm nervous, but I'll help you out. I agree."

Part 3. Trial and Terror

And so they set forth, our pure-in-heart heroes,
To voyage ahead as an unlikely trio.

They dashed through the desert (and waved to a sphinx!),
Then mounted a mountain, past yetis (who stink!).

They fled through the forest and dodged werewolves (twice!),
Then slinked through a swamp (The ogre was nice!).

The castle was finally now in their sight,
But still, up ahead, lay peril and fright.

The moat 'round the castle had crocs and piranhas.
"We could swim," shrugged Hud, "but I really don't wanna."

And as they approached, with fear in their souls,
Across the water, they spotted a troll!

"Stay back!" cried the creature (whose face was an eyeful),
"Lam has employed me to stop your arrival!"

"Now wait!" said Lil' Cap. "I get this—I see!
We just have to solve this troll's riddles three!"

"No way!" laughed the troll. "I won't draw this bridge!
I like riddles, but they don't pay my mortgage!"

Then Lil' Cap spoke up. "I've got it!" she cried,
And laid out her vision—her smile a mile wide.

"He won't draw the bridge and let us move on,
But we can take pencils and get that bridge drawn!"

The troll howled and cackled. "You three foolish nerds!
"'Drawing' and 'drawing' are two different words!"

But the princess jumped onto Foofy's big head,
And sketched out a bridge with her pencil of lead.

And once she was done, the walkway took shape!
Our heroes set forth; the troll's mouth was agape.

The troll tried to block them from moving ahead,
But Foofy snarled once and the troll quickly fled.

From there, the three outcasts approached the front gate,
Prepared to meet Lam, as well as their fate.

But right at that moment, before they could breach,
There came a distressing and deafening screech!

They looked up above, with confidence saggin',
As they met the gaze of a gigantic dragon.

Princess Lil' Cap and Sir Hud turned to Foofy,
Who shook his big head. "Well, don't look at me!"

Lil' Cap told him gently, "This is your big day.
We need you to help send this dragon away!"

But Foofy remembered being misunderstood,
And thought being kind might do everyone good.

So he didn't get mad, or start a big fight.
He just asked the dragon, "Hey, are you all right?"

That's all that it took. She sobbed and she squealed,
"No one's ever—not ever!—once asked how I feel!

"I don't like Lam either," she whined as she quaked.
"She never says 'thank you' or lets me take breaks."

"Well that isn't right!" said Hud. "That's not kind!
Join us and we'll give her a piece of our minds!"

The dragon agreed, then turned to the door,
And scorched it away with a fiery roar!

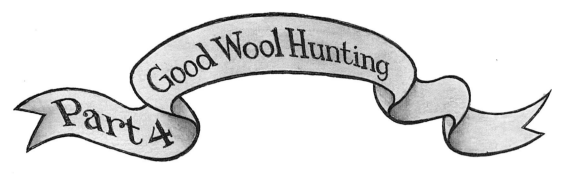

Part 4
Good Wool Hunting

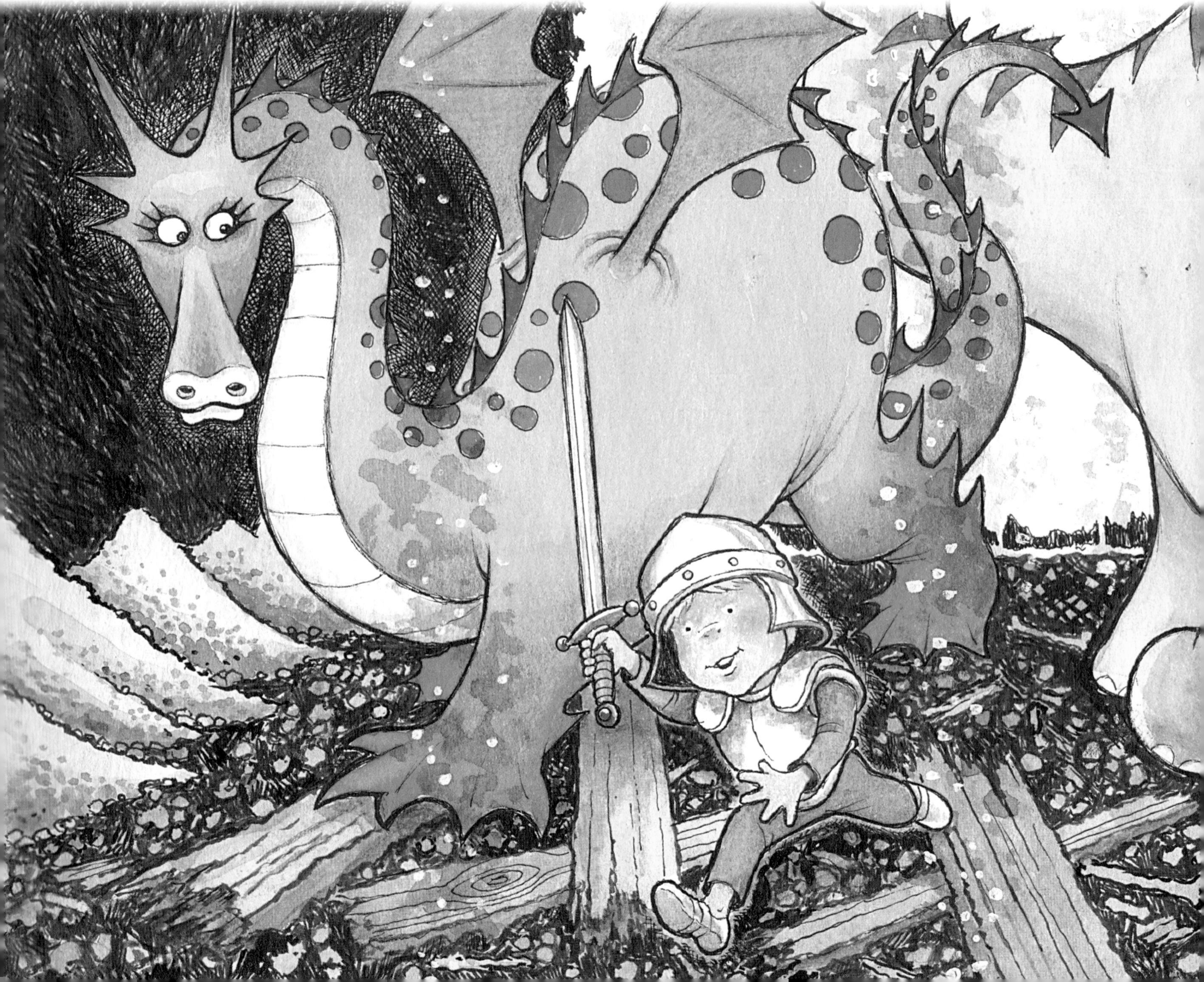

The quartet then trudged through the ash of the blast.
The time had now come...to face Lam at last.

"Come out!" yelled Sir Hud, as he banged on the door.
"We're back, with new friends. You can't hide anymore!"

And then, within seconds, to everyone's shock,
The grand chamber doors were quickly unlocked.

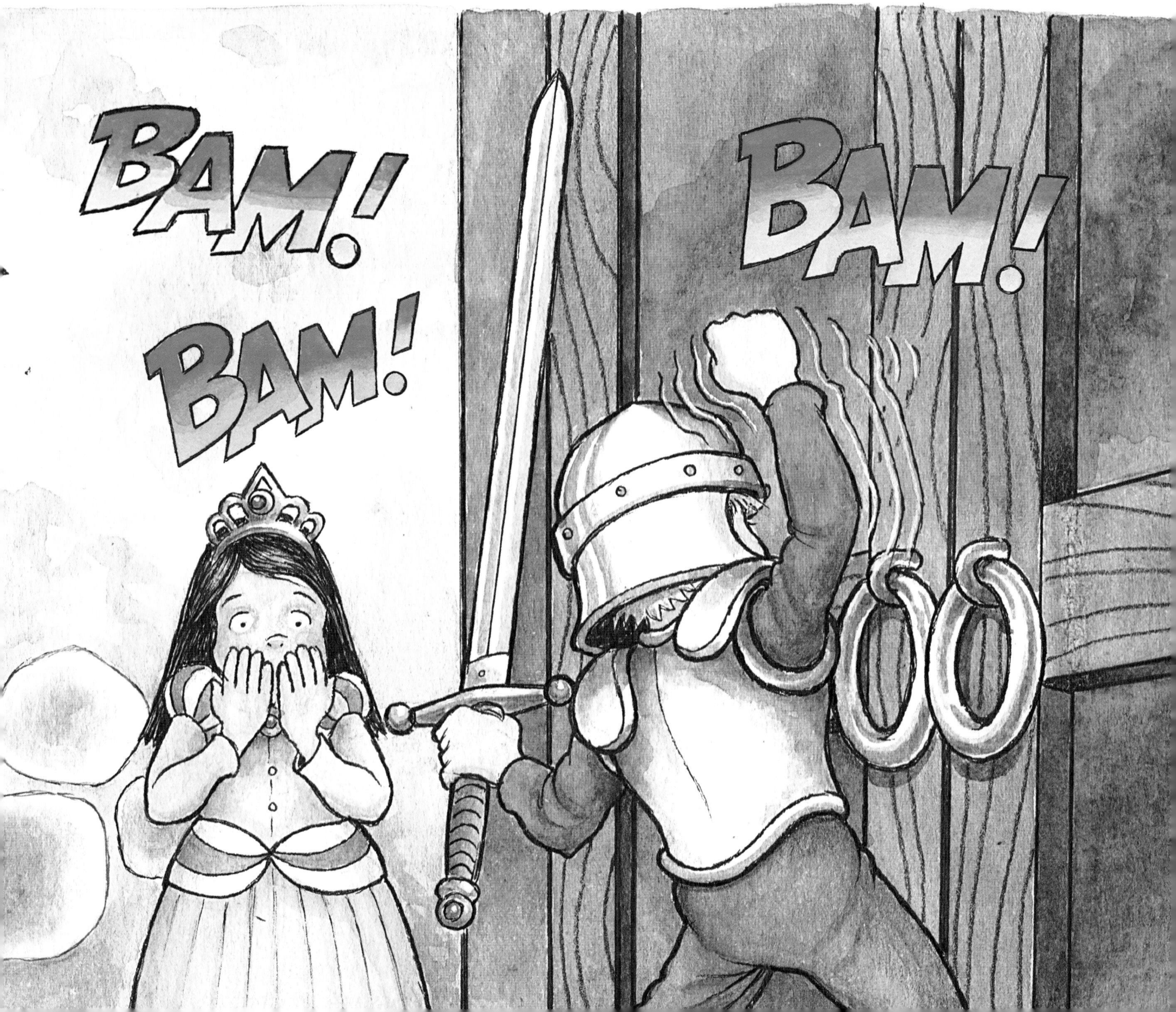
BAM!
BAM!
BAM!

"Hello," said Lambantha. "I know you're upset.
But first let me tell you...I'm full of regret.

"You didn't deserve what I did, I should say,
And the castle's been lonely with you two away.

"But if you decide to give me one more chance,
I promise to do right by you. That's my stance."

So both of them turned to the dragon, unsure,
And Princess Cap posed the question to her.

"Out of everyone here, Lam's been meanest to you.
So dragon, you tell us: What should we do?"

Cap told the tale—every turn, every twist—
So the creature could know all the details she missed.

HMMM...

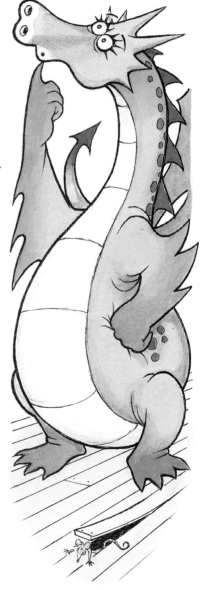

She thought long and hard about what she'd just heard,
Then said, "Just think back on the lessons you've learned.

"You've already learned to believe in yourself,
trust your wit, face your fears, and take others' help.

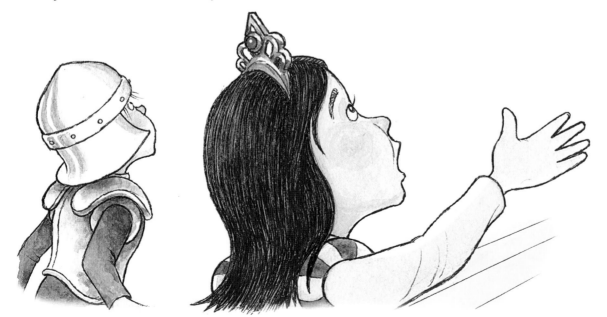

"There's just one more lesson about being brave—
And that's to forgive our friends who misbehave."

Sir Hud turned to Lam and he lowered his sword.
"We'll let you stay, if we can be assured:

"The next time you're feeling upset, out of place,
Or anything like that—tell us to our face!"

They buried the hatchet; they cleared the air.
And here's how their lives proceeded from there.

The dragon received more respect in her day job,
And guarded the castle with nary a sob.

Foofy felt comfortable facing his fears.
Now he sees dragons as approachable peers.

Lam spoke her mind more, as much as she could,
To make sure her friends always knew where she stood.

The princess kept reading each book she could get,
But also got better at trusting her wit.

And last—but not least!—there's our friend Sir Hud.
A hero. A knight. Foofy's very best bud.

For all the bold choices that this young man made,
He's earned his true title: He's Sir Hud the Brave.

Despite being different, these five understood:
To learn from each other did all of them good.

The castle halls filled with tarts, love, and laughter.
As you might've guessed: They lived happily ever after.

Acknowledgements

Like *The Little Engine That Could*, we've been chugging along on this story for years, and along the way we've picked up some helpers, just like Princess Lil' Cap and Sir Hud the Brave.

Kathryn McGarr—whose superpower is writing English gooder than we can—offered essential edits, fixed the rhythm of the verse, and added a number of whimsical touches. You have her to thank for the words "gooseberry pie" appearing in this book.

We are eternally grateful to our illustrator extraordinaire, Bill DeOre, who brought this magical world to life—and by hand! The old fashioned way!

Our children's literature guru, Robert Herrera of Pixel Mouse House Agency, brought thoughtful feedback, terrific advice, and invaluable industry experience to this process. He's the reason this book resembles a book.

This process called desperately for someone with a love for shenanigans, and we found that in HB Steadham. Her editorial work was stellar, helping us make this book the best version it could be.

Thank you, of course, to our team at Post Hill Press—including Anthony Ziccardi, Debra Englander, and Caitlin Burdette—for taking a chance on this silly little adventure and offering so much support.

We owe a lifetime of thanks to West Wing Writers, Jeff Nussbaum, and the late Brian Agler for bringing Chandler and Cappy together. My goodness, what have you done?

We also have to give a special shoutout to Admiral William H. McRaven, whose work inspired the key ethics this book is meant to impart: bravery, self-doubt, self-effacement, tenacity, honest, integrity, and forgiveness.

Finally, we would like to thank Cappy's grandkids: the real life Hudson and Annette Cap, without whom this book certainly would not exist. The events depicted in this book are fictitious, but Cappy's love for those kids is real and enduring.

Cappy McGarr is an Emmy and NAACP Image Award-nominated co-creator of the Kennedy Center Mark Twain Prize for American Humor and the Library of Congress Gershwin Prize for Popular Song. He's one of few people to be appointed by two different presidents to the Kennedy Center. His writing has been published in *The New York Times*, *The Wall Street Journal*, *Politico*, and *USA Today*—and his memoir, *The Man Who Made Mark Twain Famous*, is available at retailers everywhere.

Chandler Dean is a Brooklyn-based comedian and speechwriter whose satire has been featured in *The New Yorker*, McSweeney's, Reductress, and Hard Drive. He is a Senior Director at the speechwriting firm West Wing Writers, where he co-leads the firm's humor practice. He has also written for the Crooked Media podcast *Lovett or Leave It*, and has previously worked for *The Late Show with Stephen Colbert*, *Late Night with Seth Meyers*, and *Full Frontal with Samantha Bee*.

Bill DeOre was a nationally syndicated, award winning editorial and sports cartoonist for *The Dallas Morning News* for 34 years. His work has appeared in many newspapers, books and periodicals world-wide. He now cartoons, paints and illustrates full time, his work appearing in many novels, biographies and, of course, children's books.

GREAT
HOMES *of*
ROCHESTER *and*
the Finger Lakes

e of Richard and Jennifer Sands

Home of Tom and Linda Bell

All proceeds from the sale of this book go to benefit the following local charities:
ESL Charitable Foundation
REALTORS® Charitable Foundation (RCF)
Hillside Work-Scholarship Connection
EnCompass: Resources for Learning

Cover photograph: home of Dave and Nance Fiedler
Photography by Don Cochran; Photo Assistants: Ria Tafani-Casartelli, Jim Lyon, Jeremy Lipps
Art direction, design, and layout by Roger Winkler and Corinne Clar, Dixon Schwabl Advertising
Written by John Connelly, Dixon Schwabl Advertising

Printing provided by DPI of Rochester, LLC

ISBN # 0-9790545-0-8

First Printing: October 2006

CONTENTS

CONTENTS

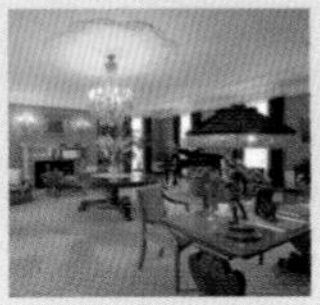

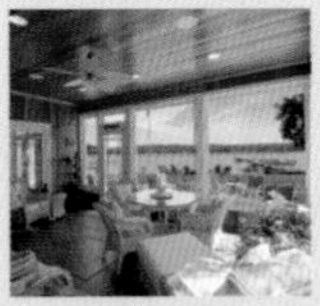

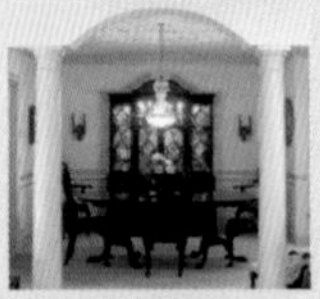

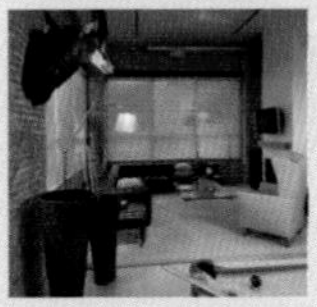

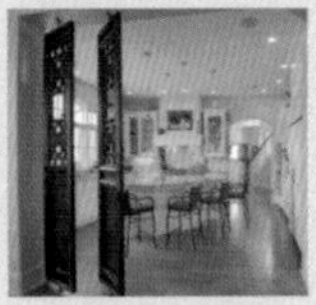

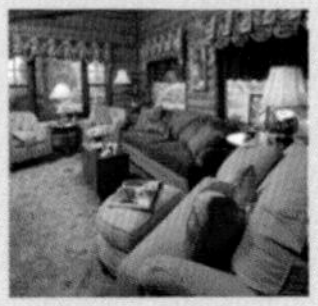

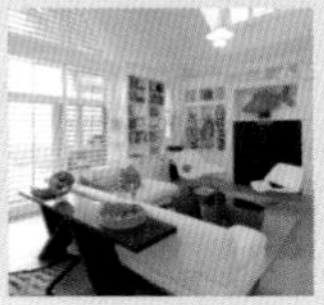

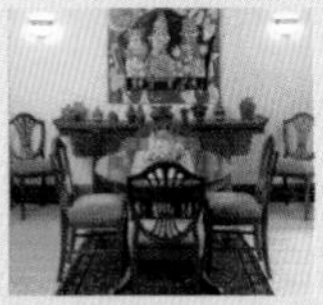

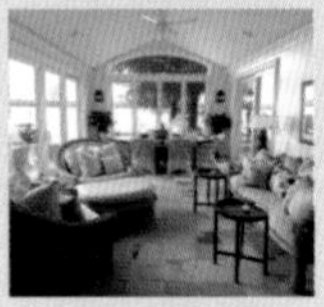

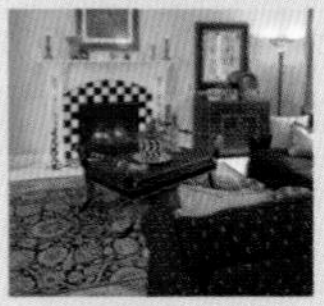

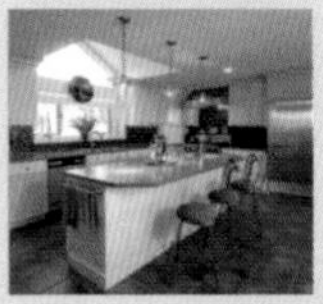

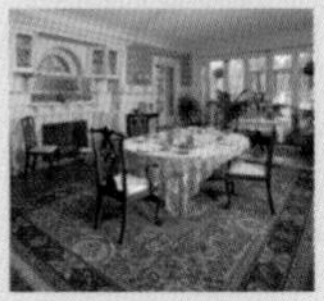

CONTENTS

An exclusive look inside some of our area's top homes.

From stately mansions to lakeside retreats, from bold new homes to historic restorations, you'll find plenty of inspiration and insight as you browse through the pages of *Great Homes of Rochester and the Finger Lakes.*

Through this open door to three dozen of our region's most spectacular residences, you'll be able to appreciate the unique talents of renowned builders, architects, interior designers, artists, and craftsmen.

It takes great people to make a great community. In these pages, you'll see the homes of many people whose names you'll recognize immediately and many others you may not know. But you can be sure that everyone in this book cares deeply about our corner of Western New York and regularly commits time, talent, and treasure to make Greater Rochester and the Finger Lakes region such a great place to live and work.

All of us at Dixon Schwabl Advertising would like to thank our friends at ESL Federal Credit Union and at Greater Rochester Association of REALTORS® for their sponsorship of this book. Without their financial support, it would never have been possible.

Home of Bruce and Linda Hellman

e of Ted and Karen Lenz

Home of Arthur and Vitoch and Margi Weggeland

Home of Henry and Cheryl Tung

DIXON SCHWABL ADVERTISING

When the idea needs to be
as big as a house, here's
the crew that can build it.

Howie Jacobson
Managing Partner

Nailing one great
home for the book
after another.

Sarah Daniels
Public Relations
Executive

Keeping focused on
new opportunities.

Lauren Dixon
CEO

If a hammer won't nail
it, try a four-inch spike.

Kara Painting
Creative Director

Making sure everything
stays on the level.

Corinne Clar
Senior Art Director/
Creative Supervisor

Finding that perfect
color for every job.

Mike Schwabl
President

When the digging
gets tough, the tough
get digging.

Joanne LaFave
Account Supervisor

Keeping everyone's
eyes on the plan.

Roger Winkler
Art Director

Setting the rules
and sticking to 'em.

John Connelly
Senior Copywriter/
Associate Creative
Director

Drilling deep for the
gold in each story.

Susan Clevenger
Executive Assistant

Making sure the book
measures up.

Paul Rizzo
Print Production
Manager

Coming through with
the finishing touch.

DIXON SCHWABL ADVERTISING

1595 Moseley Road, Victor, New York 14564   585.383.0380   www.DixonSchwabl.com

DON COCHRAN PHOTOGRAPHY

The main focus of Don Cochran's freelance business is fine architectural photography, aerial, landscape, executive portraits, and adventure sports.

Don, who lives and works in Honeoye Falls, has been a professional photographer for over a quarter century. He was a staff photographer for Eastman Kodak for 14 years, which gave him the opportunity to shoot in China, Korea, Norway, the Caribbean, and every corner of America.

His images have been published in the coffee-table book *A Day in the Life of China* and in several national and international magazines.

He shot images at the 1994 and 1996 Olympic Games and many other sporting venues. Don also taught nature photography for several summers in Rocky Mountain and Yosemite National Parks.

Many of Don's images have been appreciated by millions at the Kodak Times Square display in New York City.

Don hopes that the proceeds from the sale of this book will be a blessing to the children and families who benefit from the four charities.

For more about Don and his images, please visit www.doncphoto.com.

Can a financial institution actually inspire affection?

Happily, yes. Because providing personal touch service is our first priority. Always has been.

Always will be. Though we keep growing, we'll never lose touch with our roots. And that's a promise.

ESL is a registered service mark of ESL Federal Credit Union. Membership subject to eligibility.   585.336.1000   800.848.2265   www.esl.org

ESL
Federal Credit Union ®

It's banking, only better.

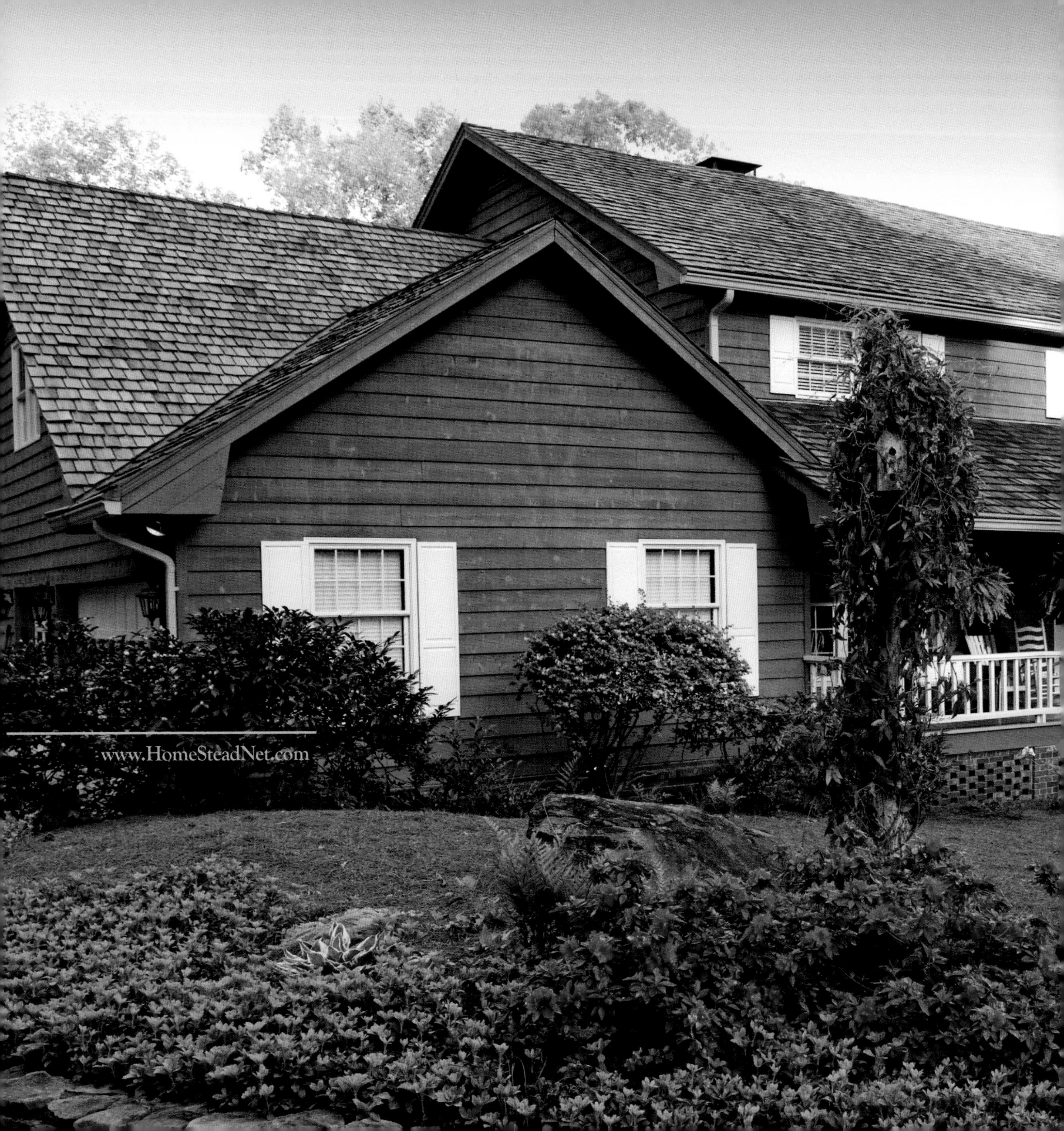
www.HomeSteadNet.com

Two-thirds of "For Sale by Owners" would use a REALTOR® the next time.

The other third swear to never, never move again.

Greater Rochester Association of **REALTORS**®

REALTORS® have the experience to price your home, so it can sell for up to 16%* more than selling it yourself. Moreover, 90% of buyers use a REALTOR® to locate a home.

Contact your local REALTOR® today and get the necessary expertise to make your buying or selling experience a positive one. And don't forget to check out the ONLY place to see ALL the local listings: **HomeSteadNet.com.**

*Based on data collected from the 2005 Profile of Homebuyers and Sellers by the National Association of REALTORS®.

Four area charities will benefit from the sale of this edition of *Great Homes of Rochester and the Finger Lakes.*

ESL CHARITABLE FOUNDATION

The ESL Charitable Foundation is dedicated to improving life in the Greater Rochester community by providing funds to a wide range of local charitable organizations and for a diverse array of projects. This Rochester-based foundation provides funding and employee volunteers to select non-profit organizations, with a primary focus on families, youth, and education.

The foundation has recently supported many area organizations, including NeighborWorks, creating opportunities for people to live in affordable homes; Golisano Children's Hospital at Strong; Hope Hall, a school serving children with special needs; Center for Youth, offering prevention education, counseling, and emergency housing; Challenger Baseball, giving children with disabilities an opportunity to participate in an organized sport; and Quad A for Kids, supporting athletic, artistic, and academic programs for inner-city students.

Home of Dave and Nance Fiedler

Home of Arthur and Vitoch and Margi Weggeland

THE REALTORS® CHARITABLE FOUNDATION

The mission of the REALTORS® Charitable Foundation (RCF), a 501(c)(3) charitable organization, is to support critical housing needs and create sustainable neighborhoods within Greater Rochester's diverse community.

Since January 2001, the RCF has made grants of over $300,000 to 26 Rochester-area not-for-profit organizations. For example, an RCF grant purchased thousands of smoke detectors that were then installed in homes by the Rochester Fire Department.

Another RCF grant helped pay for the new seven-bedroom Ronald McDonald "House Within a Hospital." This facility, which is located at the Golisano Children's Hospital at Strong, is only the fourth in the world of its kind, and the first in the Eastern U.S.

Other organizations that benefited from RCF grants include Hillside Children's Center, Wilson Commencement Park, Family Service of Rochester, Inc., Sojourner House, East House, Corn Hill Neighbors Association, Center for Youth, the YWCA, and Mercy Residential Services. For more information on the RCF, visit www.HomeSteadNet.com.

HILLSIDE WORK-SCHOLARSHIP CONNECTION

Hillside Work-Scholarship Connection was established in 1987 to help at-risk urban students stay in school and achieve academic success. Its mission is to increase the graduation rates of students within the Rochester City School District by providing long-term advocacy, academic resources, life skills development, and job training.

The program's long-range goal is to have these students become mature, self-sufficient adults who can make a genuine contribution to the Rochester community.

On average, 75% of the students who stay with Hillside Work-Scholarship Connection will graduate high school and, of these graduates, 75% to 80% will attend college and/or find gainful employment.

Hillside Work-Scholarship Connection is an affiliate of the Hillside Family of Agencies, a Rochester-based family and children services organization that provides child welfare, mental health, youth development, and developmental disabilities services across Central and Western New York.

Home of Bruce and Linda Hellman

George Eastman House

ENCOMPASS: RESOURCES FOR LEARNING

EnCompass: Resources for Learning is a 501(c)(3) not-for-profit organization that provides innovative educational services to students who struggle to learn and to the families, schools, and institutions that support them. These services are matched to each student's unique learning style in order to prevent academic failure and enhance lifelong learning.

The sources of a struggling learner's difficulties often go undetected, are undiagnosed or under-addressed. More often than not, this results in failure for the child and a loss of self-esteem. Long-term effects can be increased risk for illiteracy, dropping out of school, and even juvenile delinquency.

EnCompass' goal is to close the gap between students with learning difficulties and their peers through early identification and prevention, thereby paving the road for a lifetime of successful learning.

EnCompass was started by The Norman Howard School, which recently celebrated its 25th anniversary of serving Western New York students with learning disabilities in grades 5-12.

"Massive wood beams and detailed moldings
give our timber-framed house the inviting,
comfortable look we wanted."

Frank Steenburgh

Dreams and desires became a reality when the Steenburghs moved into their beautiful Keuka Lake home. After meeting many demolition, construction, and landscaping challenges, the stunning result is an 11-room, timber-frame residence that incorporates everything they'd ever wanted in a home. With its massive, wood-beamed ceiling, impressive chandelier, and two-story wall of custom windows, the great room is a favorite gathering place for entertaining or conversing with close friends in front of a welcoming fire.

Frank is especially proud of the temperature-controlled wine cellar he designed to house their bountiful wine collection. His wife, Fran, is equally proud of the 21-ft. high timber-framed kitchen and octagonal breakfast/dinette area. "I love how well our home was able to accommodate our favorite amenities from previous homes," she said. The Steenburghs also can't say enough about their master bedroom with its own fireplace and seating area—perfect for cozy reading on a cold winter's night.

The Steenburgh's lake home is another example of how Cutri Construction can turn a dream into reality.

Style   New England Seaside
Builder   Cutri Construction
Year Built   2004
Approximate Sq. Ft.   4,600

"From the second-floor rooms you get the feeling you're in a treehouse. It's great being so close to nature."

Charles Arena

Nestled in pristine woods high above Canadice Lake, Charles Arena found the perfect antidote from his fast-paced city life. His 1940s-era log-faced cabin sits on a three-acre plot overlooking a steep ravine with a fast-flowing creek and a series of waterfalls. "The sound of the rushing water and rustling of the hemlocks instantly relax anyone who comes here," Charles noted.

It took a dedicated seven-month restoration to bring his camp back from the run-down state he found it in. "I had a mason from Alaska use stones he found on my land to rebuild the fireplace in the living room," Charles said. His glass-walled patio provides superb views of the woods and waterfalls beyond. But Arena's favorite room is the little upstairs bathroom. "We hunted all over my property before we found the perfect log for my unique pedestal sink."

For Charles, the devil is always in the details. He and his friends took months to find the kind of woodsy, handmade furniture that would make his mountain retreat very special indeed.

Style   Adirondack Camp
Year Built   1942
Year Restored   2005
Approximate Sq. Ft.   1,100

"All our entertaining is casual. We want whoever comes
to our home to feel they can kick back and relax."

Linda Hellman

On its 70-acre site in the town of Rush, the Hellman's large French-country home offers expansive, tranquil views in all directions. Everything about this residence bespeaks the couple's good taste and insistence on uncompromising craftsmanship. They worked closely with the architect and builder to incorporate a number of design features that suited their lifestyle and ensured that every room would flow smoothly from one to another. The classic, muted colors they chose for each room added to the home's serenity.

Among the many unique design features noted by Jeffrey Smith of Woodstone Custom Homes are a barrel-vault ceiling in the foyer, custom-lathed newels and stair balusters, extensive built-in cabinetry, geothermal radiant floor heating, and specialty moldings throughout. Their exquisite home also features complete and separate living quarters on the lower level, with impressive nine-foot ceilings, an elevator to the main floor, and at-grade access to patios overlooking their spacious grounds.

Architect   Patrick J. Morabito, A.I.A.
Builder   Woodstone Custom Homes, Inc.
Style   French Country
Year Built   2001
Approximate Sq. Ft. 7,000

"Homes from the late '20s often had wonderful mouldings, built-in cabinets, and arched doorways. It's that kind of craftsmanship that makes our home special to us."

Nance Fiedler

The Fiedlers had always been huge fans of colonial revival architecture and the classic detailing which is part of an older home's charm. When, in 1997, they found a Brighton home that combined that with modern amenities, five bedrooms, the potential for wonderful gardens, and a convenient location, they knew they'd found what would become their dream home.

"While we fell in love with the potential of the house, we knew it needed a lot of work, both inside and out," Nance said. "I spent the first several years designing and building gardens in the warmer months, and designing and completing inside projects, room by room, over the winter months."

A family favorite is what the Fiedlers call their Garden Room. "Not only does it have many wonderfully unique architectural details such as the six-foot square skylight in the middle of the room," Dave said, "but it's also bright and welcoming even on the dreariest Rochester winter days."

Style   Georgian Colonial
Year Built   1930
Approximate Sq. Ft.   4,470

"Many of the contemporary homes I'd seen on the West Coast made a lasting impression on me. I wanted to bring the spirit of California living here to the shore of Lake Ontario."

Ed Pettinella

Built on a hill at the very edge of Lake Ontario, Ed's three-level home meshes seamlessly with its natural surroundings. The wide-open floor plan enables expansive, ocean-like views from virtually every room in the house, including the large master bathroom.

With a 20-ft. cathedral ceiling on the top floor, and 62 feet of Florida windows stretching from floor to ceiling, you could easily get the feeling of floating on the water. The deck just off the master bedroom is perfect for a relaxing soak in the hot tub.

Style   California
         Contemporary
Year Built   2005
Approximate Sq. Ft.   7,400

With its large, U-shaped island, the kitchen is a natural focal point when entertaining. It—and every room in the home—has rich, Brazilian cherry floors.

But the crowning glory of Pettinella's home is his 72-ft. lap/swimming pool, made all the more distinctive with illuminated fountains and a pair of waterfalls.

"Our home is warm and comfortable for the two of us, yet its open floor plan is perfect for gathering with friends and family."

Linda Bell

Though the Bell's Conesus Lake home was designed for easy living, it's clearly a feast for the eyes—from every point of view. A major feature is the stunning barrel-vault ceiling that begins as a *porte-cochere* over a heated circular driveway and continues through the great room and on to the spacious lakeside deck. A two-sided Delaware sandstone fireplace provides warmth and cozy ambiance to the living room, custom kitchen, and dining room.

Among their home's many classic touches is a wide, sweeping staircase that goes from the deck to the lake level.

As general contractor, Tom coordinated the efforts of over a dozen seasoned craftsmen to give their 11-room home the welcoming character and great views of the finest New England beach houses with the refinement perfectly suited to their large collection of original art.

Builder   Tom Bell
Style   New England Coastal
Year Built   1998
Approximate Sq. Ft.   5,500

"The site of the house, its many windows and skylights, and its open floor plan provide constantly changing views, bringing nature into our comfortable inside world."

Diane Berlyn

The spectacular view overlooking Keuka Lake, 1000 feet above sea level, was reason enough for the Berlyns to choose this 12-acre site for their dream home.

As artists, conservators, and retired teachers who still worked on a professional level, the Berlyns were looking for a home design that would enable them to pursue their careers in the same space where they could live comfortably. "We wanted something that would suit us esthetically and still serve us

practically," Sheldon said. "The timber frame design Al Millanette came up with did both—and beautifully," he added. Sheldon made a major contribution to the project by designing the home's main stairway and balcony railings.

The couple loves how their home's large glass windows provide them with sensational views of the ever-changing lake and hills beyond. "But with a home like ours, it's really all about the wood," Diane said.

Builder   Timber Frames, Inc.
Style   Timber Frame
Year Built   2001
Approximate Sq. Ft.   4,100

AUTUMN

"Because this is a very open house,
it's great for entertaining.
Whether the gathering is large or small
you'd hardly know the difference."

Don Alhart

Don and Mary Alhart are glad they listened to their architect at the blueprint stage. "He told us big windows and lots of them were very important in this part of the country, where gray skies are the norm," Mary said.

One of the other great ideas he included in the design was the butler's pantry that is off the dining room and only a few steps from the kitchen. "It's an ideal staging area for parties," Don noted, "and a real lifesaver at holiday times when we have a houseful of guests."

Don told us their Penfield home has a comfortable nesting quality to it. There is plenty of room for collectibles they've amassed over a lifetime of travels.

The Alharts are well known for their sense of humor. "We have two 'On the Air' signs here. One, appropriately, is just outside my at-home studio. The other," Don said, "is more for laughs; it goes on whenever someone's using the powder room that's off our family room."

Style   Transitional
Year Built   1993
Approximate Sq. Ft.   4,400

"Our home is a little on the wild side!
It's very whimsical and fun!"
Lauren Dixon

Lauren and Mike's Canandaigua Lake home is bold and bright and energetic! It's filled with commissioned art works and furniture by many of our area's most talented artists: Wendell Castle, MacKenzie-Childs, Nancy Gong, Paul Knoblauch, Elizabeth Lyons, and Scott Grove.

"It's great to fill your home with art you love and even better when you know the artists personally," Mike said.

"Everyone thought we were crazy to have four ovens and two kitchens, but we entertain all the time. We have four children and we subscribe to the 4-F's... 'Forced Family Fun on Fridays.' All the kids have to stay home on Fridays, but the rule is that they can invite as many kids to stay overnight as they'd like! Saturday morning breakfasts are a blast," Lauren said.

Architect   James Fahy, P.E.
Builder   Ketmar Development Corporation
Style   Contemporary
Year Remodeled   2004
Approximate Sq. Ft.   7,000

35

Builder   Ketmar Development Corporation

"Every time I look around our home
I'm amazed at the quality of the workmanship
that went into making every room special."
Cheryl Tung

The Tung's stately 15-room home in Pittsford is the result of two years of planning. The couple reviewed hundreds of home décor magazines, clipping pictures of design elements they wanted to incorporate into their dream home.

The stunning result is an open floor plan that suits their family's active lifestyle. The family room's elegant coffered ceiling and French-style stone fireplace and the foyer's floating circular staircase reflect the home's European inspiration. The Old World character is also carried out in such exterior elements as the

castle stone, limestone trim and balusters, copper finials, arched-top roof vents, and hand-forged, wrought-iron front door.

A real eye-opener is the Tung's theater room, with its cinema-themed carpet with popcorn boxes and film reels. "It's perfect for family movie nights," Henry says, "with big, comfortable reclining chairs, complete with cup holders." Sounds like a fun place to hang out on weekends.

Architect Patrick J. Morabito, A.I.A.
Builder Ketmar Development Corporation
Kitchen Custom Kitchens by Martin and Co., Inc.
Style European Chateau
Year Built 2006
Approximate Sq. Ft. 7,750

"We love how the design and colors
of our new home blend in so well
with the wooded surroundings."
Lori Van Dusen

After living in an older house on this site for ten years, Lori and Ron had come up with many ways to make their new Kuras home better suit their family's lifestyle—and make the most of their wooded hillside lot.

One architectural element that sets this home apart is the completely round turret. The couple can enjoy magnificent views of Canandaigua Lake from their spacious master bedroom suite on the turret's upper level.

Impressive stonework abounds. The great room and kitchen feature a stunning natural slate floor. Since the slate pieces varied greatly in thickness, many had to be built up to create a flat floor. Native pond stone is used in their fireplaces. In the master bath, much of the limestone features fossilized shells.

For gracious fair-weather entertaining, the home features large decks on two levels and a fixed deck and dock at the water's edge.

Builder   Kuras Construction Corp.

Style   Contemporary

Year Built   2005

Approximate Sq. Ft.   3,600

"Many area artisans worked on this project, making our home even more special."

Dianne Eichel

The Eichel's Pittsford home was designed by one of the most famous architects of the Arts & Crafts period, Ward Wellington Ward. While they needed to enlarge the home substantially to fit their lifestyle, the Eichels insisted on an addition that would tie in flawlessly with the home's classic 1920s design. The year-long, 1200 sq. ft. renovation gave them a spacious family room, kitchen, dining area, computer room, and a three-car garage. Outside, they added a handsome slate-slab patio with a magnificent koi pond and two-tiered waterfall.

The new family room's mahogany built-in benches and bookshelves, mantel, doors, and trim complement the dark woods found throughout the house. The kitchen features custom-built mahogany cabinetry with leaded-glass windows and wonderful mosaics—designed and cut by homeowner Dianne Eichel—depicting flowers, birds, insects, and fish. A significant part of their home renovation was the complete transformation of their third floor to an elegant, loft-style bedroom suite.

Architect Patrick J. Morabito A.I.A.

Builder Mazzarella & Cannan

Style English Tudor

Year Built 1926

Approximate Sq. Ft. 4,500

41

Architect J. Foster Warner

"Fittingly, the home of the world's leading
 promoter of photography was restored
with the extensive aid of photographs."

Frank Donegan

The founder of Eastman Kodak Company built what the British would call a "stately home" between 1902 and 1905. When the imposing 50-room Colonial Revival mansion was completed, it was—and still is—the largest single-family residence in Monroe County. He had created more than just a fireproof building made of reinforced concrete. In the process, he oversaw the construction of a unique urban estate complete with ten-and-a-half acres of working farm land, exquisite formal gardens, greenhouses, stables, barns, and pastures.

The residence and its furnishings cost $500,000, which may sound like a bargain today. But back in 1905, this was truly a princely sum, considering $5 per day was the average living wage.

Always an innovator, Eastman ensured that his home had every "modern" convenience including state-of-the-art central heating, an electrical generator, an internal telephone system with 21 stations, a built-in vacuum cleaning system, a central clock network, an elevator, and a superb pipe organ.

Style   Colonial Revival

Year Built   1905

Approximate Sq. Ft.   35,000

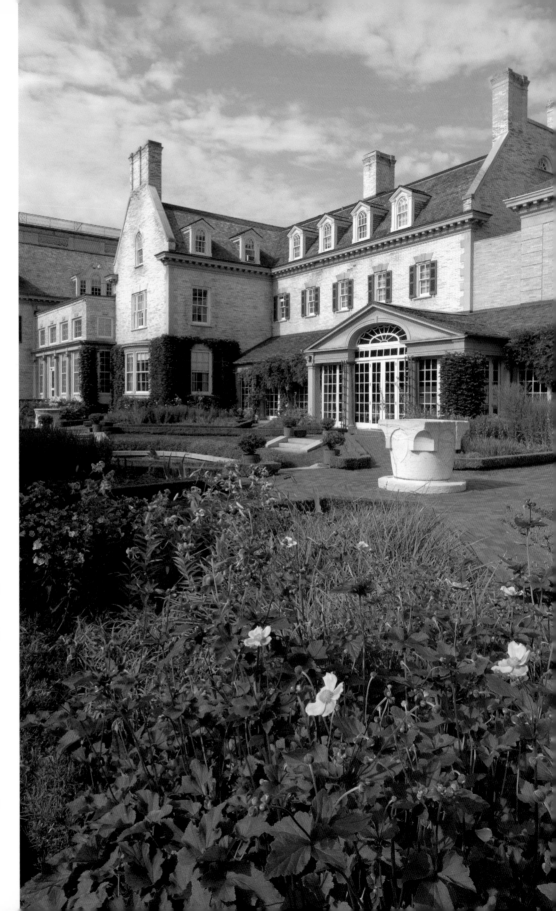

In 1919, Eastman decided that enlarging the conservatory would make this organ sound better. He had the house sliced in half and stretched a little over nine feet; this work alone cost more than the original house itself. But it was worth the expense as, he felt, it improved the proportions of the room.

Unlike other very rich people of his era, George Eastman was not fond of antiques. Rather, he chose custom-made Sheraton, Hepplewhite, and American Empire reproductions for his home, most made by the A. H. Davenport Company in Boston. His taste in paintings was also conservative. Of the more than 200 paintings he had purchased for his home, many were by such masters as Rembrandt, Tintoretto, and Gainsborough. These highly prized originals were later given to Rochester's Memorial Art Gallery.

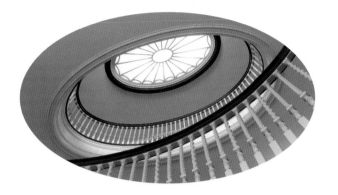

Eastman's mansion opened to the public as a museum in 1949. By January 1990, a meticulous 14-month restoration had been completed at a cost of $1.7 million. A remarkable 85 percent of the furniture now on display is original to the house, painstakingly reupholstered or refinished for authenticity. The home and its five gardens are a National Historic Landmark.

George Eastman's original house and the buildings attached to it also comprise the world's oldest photography museum and one of the world's largest film archives, housing more than 27,000 film titles produced between 1895 and the present in climate-controlled vaults.

"Now, with a larger house and an open floor plan,
it's easier than ever to entertain family and friends.
And enjoy the beauty of the lake."

Kim Dougherty

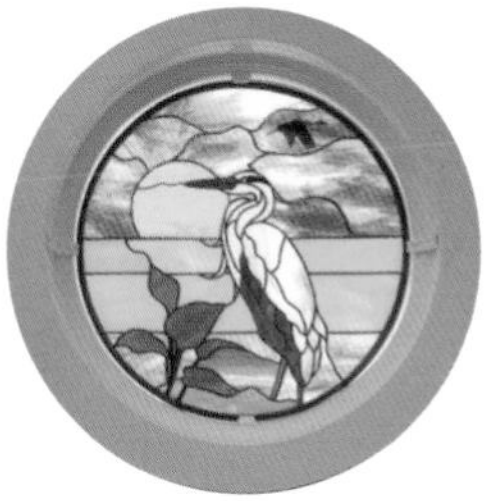

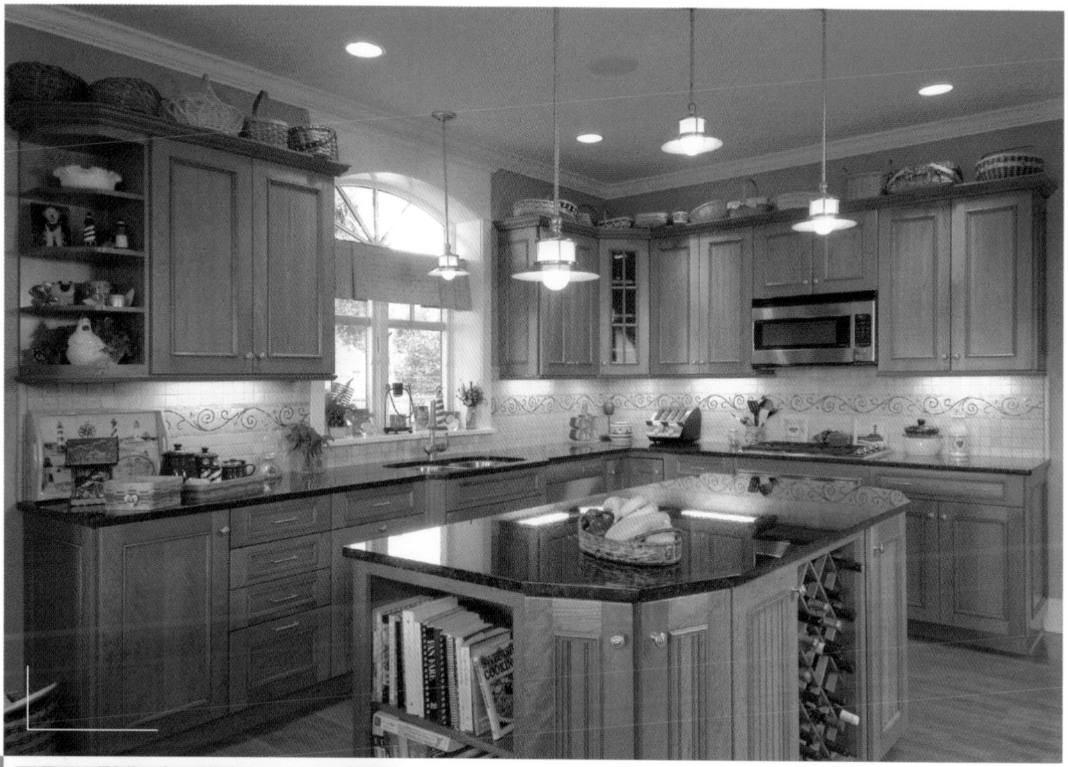

Prior to building this, their dream home, Kim and Jerry had a summer-only cottage on the same lot. "We decided several years ago that we wanted to build our retirement home right here, because this location holds so many family memories for us," Jerry said.

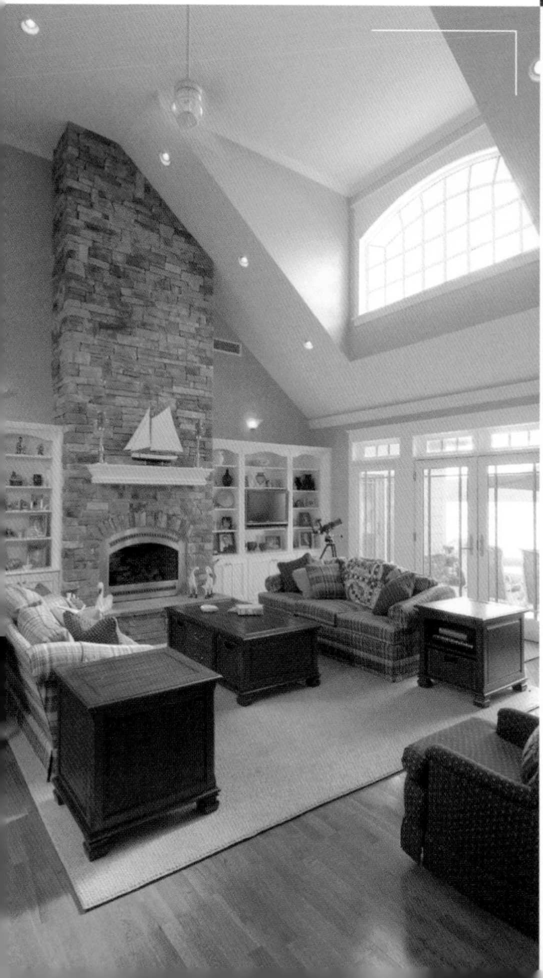

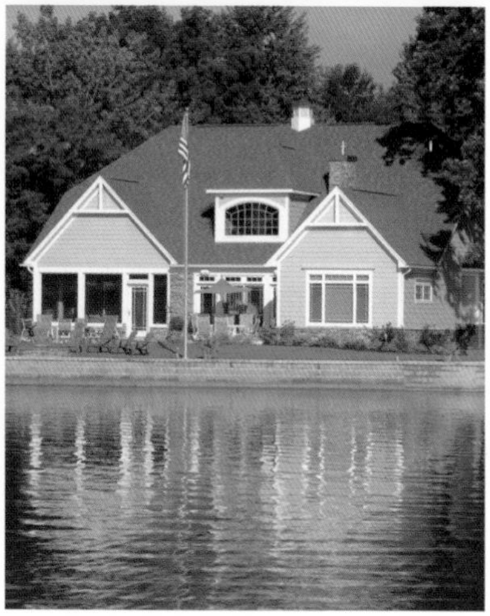

The Doughertys collected ideas from many model homes and had their architect do his best to blend them. They wanted openness and views of the lake from three sides of the house. "Putting it all on a pie-shaped lot was only one of the challenges we gave him," Kim added.

One of their favorite rooms for all but the coldest months is the three-season porch with large, lake-facing screened windows. When the weather turns chilly, the screens are replaced with glass, gaining the family more months to enjoy their marvelous view of Conesus Lake. Another favorite room is the home's great room. "It turned out to be both cozy and spacious, thanks to a high ceiling and a stone fireplace that reaches a second-story height."

Architect Mark P. Muller
Builder Bernhardt's Remodeling Center
Style Shingle-Style Lakefront
Year Built 2006
Approximate Sq. Ft. 4,400

KEVIN and BETH WILLIAMS

"The memories that we treasure
are created with those who gather here."

Beth Williams

48

Kevin and Beth Williams knew what they wanted in their custom home. They first searched for the right land with abundant trees and wildlife on a quiet street. "The process took nearly two years," Kevin recalled. "We then spent another year finalizing the design of our house."

Beth provided most of the planning behind the home's design. "We visited several model homes, combined amenities that suited our lifestyle, and created a pencil drawing of the floorplan for our architect to transform." The result is a home that is modern yet has many touches you'd expect in a home from the '30s or '40s: arched windows and walls, vaulted ceilings, stately columns, a sweeping staircase. "We wanted to avoid right angles in the footprint of the house. Bay windows and alcoves off the central core make our home open, spacious, and welcoming."

Kevin required a wing separate from the home's living area to accomodate his meteorological forecasting and research business. He said, "My 'commute' to deliver morning-drive weather reports on radio stations throughout the U.S. and Canada has been a 'breeze'...just two flights of stairs."

Style   Traditional
Year Built   1994
Approximate Sq. Ft.   4,500

49

"After spending long hours in restaurant kitchens with eight or nine foot ceilings, it's great to come home to ceilings almost twice as tall."

Tony Gullace

The owner of three area restaurants—Max of Eastman Place, Max Chophouse, and Max at the Lake—Tony Gullace found the kind of place that makes the most of city living. "This loft could just have well been transplanted from Tribeca or SoHo." Tony said. "You just can't beat the sense of space."

Tony loves the dramatic skyline views he gets through his flat's huge windows. He worked with several well-respected interior designers to perfect the cosmopolitan look he was after. One of his prized possessions—proudly situated right off his living room—is a

handsome billiard table that's well over 100 years old. "What makes it even more special to me," Tony said, "was that it was manufactured right here in Rochester."

A purist at heart, Tony doesn't like clutter. So he chose several large graphic elements to fill the large spaces throughout his loft. "In my dining room, for instance, an eight-foot-square painting and ten-foot-long chandelier did the trick," he said.

Style   Loft Apartment
Year Built   Late 19th Century
Approximate Sq. Ft.   1,400

"We built this home to suit our empty-nester lifestyle.

The open plan and flowing spaces are a key part of it."

Stacey Haralambides

Stacey applied his skills as an architect and builder to create a residence that would be more at home in Tuscany than on a Perinton hilltop. The high ceilings, flowing spaces, muted colors, rounded corners on walls and arches, large yet simple moldings, extra thick walls, and stonework definitely set a Mediterranean mood.

The most striking feature of the house is the large space that flows smoothly from a lounge with a stone fireplace to a wet bar to an open dining space and on to a very spacious kitchen.

A pair of antique wooden Chinese door panels swivel 90 degrees to either open up or close off the kitchen from the main dining area.

One of Stacey's design challenges was to give them the privacy to enjoy their patio and pool without blocking the view of the adjacent golf course and the woods beyond. "The right combination of berms, fencing, and landscaping gave us the result we were looking for."

Architect Stacey Haralambides, A.I.A.
Buider The Aristo Company
Style Tuscan Influence
Year Built 2002
Approximate Sq. Ft. 4,000

"We wanted a home that would instill some balance and fit our gardening lifestyle. Here, we've found harmony in our home, our gardens, and our day-to-day life."

Frances Grossman

Larry and Frances' lifestyle is casual, warm, and unpretentious. Their genuine log home reflects who they are and immediately puts their guests at ease.

Situated on what was once a ten-acre cornfield, their home was a labor of love. It was first designed by Larry and then he oversaw every phase of its construction. The trees and gorgeous gardens that surround the house were designed and created by Larry as well.

In the summer, the Grossmans love their front porch, back patio, and the "secret" patio off their master bedroom. "Casual, comfortable

outdoor furnishings and a fire pit invite us to live outdoors as much as we can," Frances said. "We use these spaces as an extension of our home."

In the winter, the loft is where the couple finds themselves the most. As Larry put it, "The warmth from the wood stove and coziness from the wood beams beckons us to unwind. It's both a sanctuary and a hibernation 'cave' at the same time."

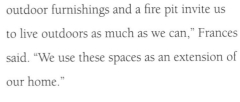

Style   Log Home
Year Built   1983
Approximate Sq. Ft.   2,400

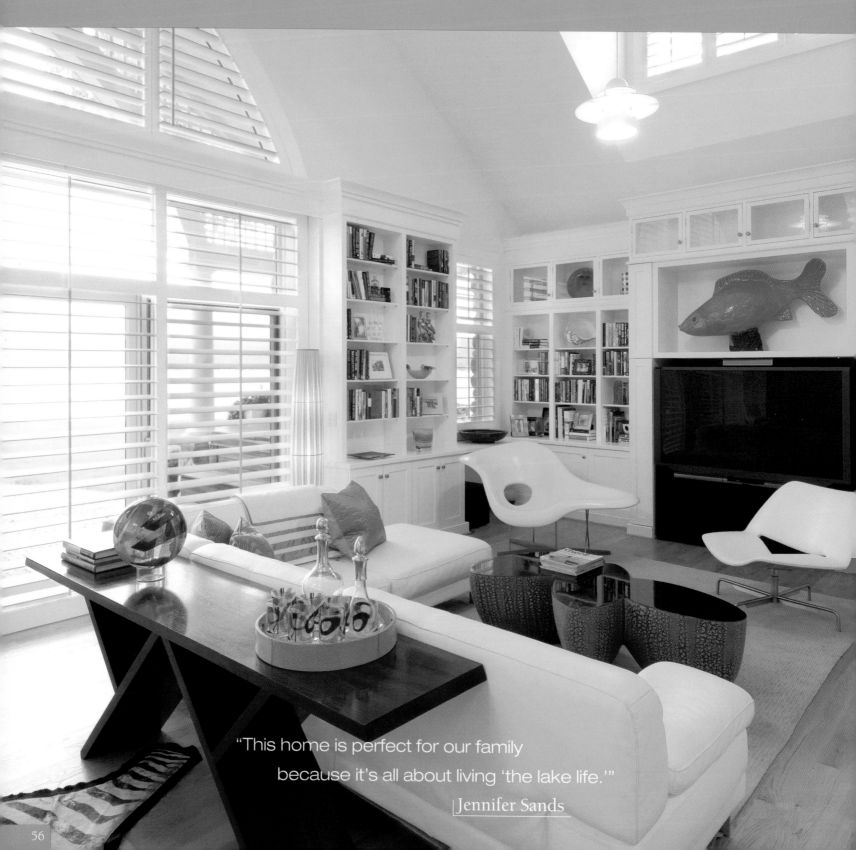

"This home is perfect for our family because it's all about living 'the lake life.'"

Jennifer Sands

Virtually every room in Richard and Jennifer Sands' spectacular Canandaigua Lake home is a sensory delight. If it isn't the arches and post-and-beam construction in one room that grabs you, then it will be the vaulted ceilings and huge glass walls in another.

One feature the Sands love in their home is the screened-in porch between the main house and the guest quarters. "It provides a great communal eating area and meeting place," Jennifer said, "but gives our kids—and frequent guests—a separate 'house' of their own. That's perfect for lake living."

The goal of increasing the family's living space became a reality when the Sands bought the property next door. Richard and Jennifer knew that with six kids of their own—and future generations to come—they would always have a need for extra breathing space. "With this house and a magnificent 17-mile-long lake at our doorstep, there's plenty of room for everyone to do their own thing," Richard said.

Style   New England Oceanfront
Year Renovated   2003
Approximate Sq. Ft.   7,000

"People know us for our dinner parties.
With our bigger kitchen and restaurant-grade appliances,
we can tackle any of them in style."

Maria Friske

Coffeehouse owner "Java Joe" Palozzi and artist Maria Friske enjoy the convenience of city living. "With a couple of entrepreneurial businesses, we're both running all the time. We needed a place that worked with our fast-paced lifestyle," Maria said.

Their home, between Cobbs Hill and Highland Parks, is a colorful, eclectic environment, a refuge of sorts, surrounded by Maria's paintings and artistic works from primitive Tiano and southern jug pottery to African masks.

Their nine-room home also serves as Maria's art studio, one part in their finished attic, and a three-season studio behind the house. When she wasn't busy painting on canvas, Maria painted every wall in their house, many with a rag-off/glaze technique that she had perfected.

A major improvement came when the couple enlarged the kitchen and opened it up to the dining room. "We wanted these rooms set up so we could cook big and cook great," Maria added.

Style   Colonial
Year Built   1920s
Approximate Sq. Ft.   1,800

"We love the openness and livability of our home.
It's situated to give us the privacy we want as well as
views of the lake from every room. And it's great for entertaining."

Seana Holtz

When John and Seana purchased their Canandaigua Lake home in the mid-'80s, they knew they'd have to make substantial changes for it to meet their needs. "Even though it had been remodeled many times since the late 19th century, its floor plan didn't flow the way we wanted it to," Seana said.

The goal of their 1987 renovation was to open up the house and give each room a lake view. "That was a major accomplishment," John said, "but by 2003 we were ready to make more changes." Initially they thought about enlarging their breakfast room and screening in a deck but opted for the versatility of a year-round sunroom instead. "With its large glass surfaces on three walls, cathedral ceiling, and wonderful lake views, this room is definitely one of our favorites," Seana added.

The Holtzes also love the Far East flavor of their living room, highlighted by massive Asian temple doors that frame the large floor-to-ceiling windows and handmade Philippine bamboo chaise lounges flanking the fireplace.

Style   Transitional
Year Built   Late 1800s
Remodeled   1987 and 2003
Approximate Sq. Ft.   4,560

61

"Our home reflects our passion for entertaining, and enjoying special times with friends and family."

Ginny Clark

With its open floor plan—and a large patio, mosaic-trimmed outdoor bar, and in-ground pool—the Clark's home in Mendon is ideal for entertaining, inside and out. The home's colorful décor features the work of MacKenzie-Childs and of such noted artists as Lorri Parker and Paul Knoblauch.

In the great room, Ginny collaborated with Parker on the creative treatment for the fireplace surround. With inspiration from MacKenzie-Childs, they used broken shards of pottery to create a mosaic on the fireplace front, then painted the tiles black and white to complete the effect.

The dining room is one of the family's favorite areas of the house, with its recessed ceiling, bold colors, and custom-designed chairs.

In addition to creating an indoor environment that is warm and inviting, the Clarks carried their love of color to the outdoors by creating impressive hillside landscaping on their two-acre site.

Style   Colonial
Year Built   2002
Approximate Sq. Ft.   3,650

"We wanted a spacious yet cozy home, lake views from every room, and almost no interior walls. Somehow, our architect found a way to do it."

Mary Maida

areas, he used architectural columns, changed the direction of the wood flooring, chose a different floor surface altogether, or simply varied the ceiling height to separate one room from another.

When entertaining, the couple especially enjoys their bright, spacious, well-equipped kitchen and its sensational views of Canandaigua Lake.

When Mary and Dave brought in a three-inch-thick binder showing all the features they hoped their architect could work into their home design, they thought he'd pass out. "We also wanted him to incorporate the best of what we enjoyed in the other homes in which we'd lived," Mary said.

One of their prime goals was a very open floor plan. To create distinctly separate rooms without having walls, the architect used various design elements. The sunroom, for instance, is defined by a high octagonal tray ceiling, corresponding octagonal floor inlays, and a large leather sectional sofa. In other

Style   Eclectic
Year Built   1999
Approximate Sq. Ft.   6,000

"The more you walk around the property,
the better you appreciate how well Sonnenberg
lives up to its German translation: "Sunny Hill.""

Jim Ingalls, Director

Few homes in New York State rival the classic elegance of Sonnenberg, Frederick and Mary Thompson's mansion and gardens in Canandaigua.

This 40-room estate—one of five homes owned by the founder of Citibank and his wife—has the steeply pitched roofs, numerous balconies, turrets, towers, gables, bays, and large verandas that are typical of Queen Anne-style mansions.

The mansion was built of rusticated graystone and features Medina sandstone trim, half-timber gables, and a genuine slate roof.

On the inside of the mansion, one can see a dazzling array of balconies, arches, landings, niches, bays, leaded and plain glass, and an intriguing combination of beamed, coved, and plain ceilings. The Thompsons included some features in this home that were very rare for the 1880s, most notably that each bedroom had its own fireplace, bathroom, and balcony. Many of the home's windows were designed to provide cross-breezes, especially useful in the century before air conditioning.

Style   Queen Anne
Year Built   1887
Approximate Sq. Ft.   40,000

67

Since the mansion was designed to have central heating—exceedingly rare for its time—the doors on the first floor could be eliminated. This gave the estate an unusual sense of spaciousness.

After Mrs. Thompson passed away in 1923, the Sonnenberg estate was willed to her nephew, Emory Clark; he sold it to the U.S. Government eight years later. Prior to the sale, nearly all the mansion furnishings were either taken by family

members, sold at auction, or given away. The furnishings in Sonnenberg today are largely the result of generous gifts and loans. These have been combined with whatever original pieces could be located and returned.

Once encompassing some 200 acres, Sonnenberg Gardens & Mansion State Historic Park currently covers an impressive 50 acres and includes nine magnificent gardens.

"The lake's spirit permeates
our looking glass through the seasons...
ever changing, ever the same."

Marie Kenton

The Kenton's dream was to have a Canandaigua Lake home that would blend into its natural surroundings yet be as close to the lake as possible. They were able to realize the first part of their dream when they found a plot of land that had once served as a loading dock for area farmers. That enabled them to build their Adirondack-inspired home just a few yards away from the water's edge.

Ask anyone who lives on a lake and they'll tell you it's all about the view. The Kentons devised a unique exterior pocket-door system that virtually brings the outdoors inside. Their combined kitchen and hearth room—where they cook, dine, and entertain—offers truly panoramic views up and down the lake.

To add to the 11-room house's rustic character, Charlie and Marie have incorporated a great deal of reclaimed timber, inside and out. Unique balcony railings, crafted entirely out of rebar, resemble grape vines in winter.

Architect   James Fahy, P.E.

Builder   Ketmar Development Corporation

Kitchen   Custom Kitchens by
           Martin and Co., Inc.

Style   Adirondack/Lake

Year Built   2003

Approximate Sq. Ft.   5,850

"I wanted a home that integrates classic design elements yet would meet the demands of an always-evolving family."

John Colaruotolo

You only have to spend a few moments in this house to appreciate its innovative use of space, especially on its first floor. After many years of designing and building homes, Anco's John Colaruotolo is convinced that modern families naturally gravitate to one area of the home for meals, to synchronize schedules, discuss homework and chores, or simply to reconnect with each other at the end of the day. He calls this space The Culinary Stage™ and it has become a major focus in all his home designs.

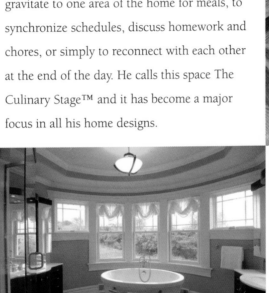

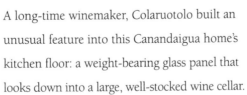

Builder   Anco Builders, LLC
Style   Contemporary / Traditional
Year Built   2006
Approximate Sq. Ft.   4,100

A long-time winemaker, Colaruotolo built an unusual feature into this Canandaigua home's kitchen floor: a weight-bearing glass panel that looks down into a large, well-stocked wine cellar.

Another notable feature of this 11-room home is just off the spacious kitchen. A flexible space—he calls it the Swing Room—may start out as a playroom, be easily converted to a media center or homework area, and can eventually become a formal dining room.

"Even though we're just a Tiger Woods' drive
from the village, our pool and the woods behind it
make us feel like we're a world away."

Rob Sands

With its 50-foot pool, a white brick cabana with wet bar and exotic anigre wood cabinetry, and pergolas wrapped in grape vines and wisteria, visitors to the Sands' home might think they'd time-traveled to Southern California. The cabana was built to match the classic lines of their adjacent 7,000-sq.-ft. Country French home. "With guests coming to visit us from around the world, it's great to have

Builder Cutri Construction
Style Country French/Ranch
Outdoor Remodeling 2005
Approximate Sq. Ft. 7,000

a roomy place to entertain them," Nancy said. "Or give them comfortable surroundings if they're staying for a few days."

A favorite year-round gathering place in their 25-room Pittsford home is a kind of indoor patio. It features a massive stone fireplace, an indoor barbecue, complete entertainment center, and plush leather seating.

Rob especially enjoys spending time in his study and library. "I love the warmth of the coppered wallpaper on the vaulted ceiling and built-in rosewood cabinetry," he said. "And the red limestone floor completes the picture."

"A lot of the inspiration for our home's
new look came from ski lodges
we've frequented in the Rocky Mountains."

Karen Lenz

For over 30 years, Ted and Karen Lenz have shared a passion for gardening. Their property, on Canandaigua Lake, has given them an idyllic setting for a spectacular home and the many gardens that surround it.

Among their home's many transitions, the most notable one for them was the 1996 renovation that brought the façade nearly twenty feet closer

to the lake. With a wall that's virtually all windows, it gives the home a sense of openness that virtually brings the outdoors inside.

One of Karen's favorite pastimes is having her morning coffee on the second-story indoor balcony that's just outside the master bedroom suite. The higher vantage point offers a marvelous view of the lake, no matter what the season.

Ted and Karen also find the spacious kitchen's open plan ideal for entertaining. "The way it flows into the great room, a large deck, and a screened-in gazebo enables our guests to socialize in whatever space suits them best," Karen said.

Style   Contemporary/Traditional
Year Remodeled   1996
Approximate Sq. Ft.   4,000

"Living up to our Italian heritage, we're known for great food and having large family get-togethers. That's why we're glad we can seat 24 people at our dining room table."

Mario Daniele

Local restaurateur Mario Daniele and his wife, Flora, have lived in their suburban home for nearly 30 years. "We love our Pittsford neighborhood," Mario said. "And the location is perfect for our busy lifestyles. It's less than 15 minutes from our restaurants: Mario's Italian Steak House and Bazil Restaurants."

On an equally practical note, Flora loves her home's layout, especially how her kitchen and the family room flow into one another.

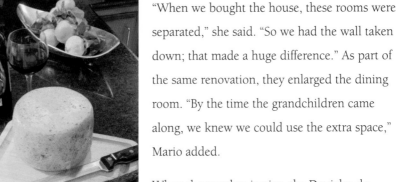

"When we bought the house, these rooms were separated," she said. "So we had the wall taken down; that made a huge difference." As part of the same renovation, they enlarged the dining room. "By the time the grandchildren came along, we knew we could use the extra space," Mario added.

When the weather is nice, the Danieles do much of their entertaining outdoors, taking full advantage of their spacious deck, patio, and large backyard.

Style   Traditional
Year Built   1972
Approximate Sq. Ft.   3,000

"From complete restorations to the smallest individual decorative tile, we have—or can get—what people need to make their homes a showplace."
Judy Shambo, President

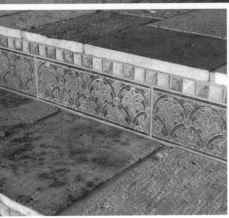

Tile, stone, and mosaic surfaces have been beautifying residences and buildings of stature for well over four millennia. They're found in the oldest pyramids, and in ancient ruins throughout the former Greek, Roman, and Byzantine empires. And, when centuries of dust were removed, these surfaces still looked as good as new.

Our congratulations to the majority of homeowners in this book who not only appreciated the beauty and value of tile and stone but who have also found everything that would set their homes apart at The Tile Room.

For over 20 years, when interior designers, architects, and discriminating homeowners from across Upstate New York wanted to create a distinctive, custom look in a kitchen or bath—or virtually any part of the home—they've put The Tile Room at the top of their "must-visit" list.

"We can't imagine not waking up to this view every day. It's like being on vacation 365 days a year."

Arthur Vitoch

Having grown up on Eastern Long Island, Arthur Vitoch has long known the pleasures of year-round waterfront living. For over 15 years, his and Margi's labor of love and perennial work in progress has been their casual and eclectic home on Lake Ontario. Pleasantly tucked away and off the beaten path in Summerville, the home has become a showcase of Arthur's many artistic talents. It's also a wonder of visual surprises with its cathedral and open-beam ceilings, a pergola-covered deck, and wide-open, handsomely appointed living spaces.

Adjacent to the main house, there is a guest cottage and Arthur's studio, aptly nicknamed "The West Wing."

Just as you might expect with a noted interior designer, the home takes on a completely different character as winter approaches. The living room furniture's white canvas slipcovers come off and the summer's cobalt blue rug is stored, to be replaced with an oriental rug and furniture with rich cream and red tones.

Style   Nantucket Beach House
Year Remodeled   Ongoing
Approximate Sq. Ft.   3,000

"My favorite room is always the last room that I complete."
Louis Perticone

Ask art collector Louis Perticone how he would characterize his eclectic living space and he'll tell you it's a series of unique American environments of the 20th century. His apartment was the first part of what would become Artisan Works, a Rochester museum and major attraction for art aficionados from across the country.

Louis' Tatami dining room, with its shoji screens, low table, and *objets d'art,* is pure Japanese. His combined living room/bedroom suite is what you'd expect in a SoHo loft. You'll find

Perticone's homage to the Arts & Crafts era is his mission-style kitchen. With its wide-open floor plan and ceilings that reach 33 feet, Louis says he never fears claustrophobia.

His home is topped with a remarkable rooftop sculpture garden unlike any other. Anywhere.

"My dream was to create experiences for people who come to visit the museum," Louis says. "I've been creating environments since I was a kid. In many ways, I still am a kid."

Style It's an Environment
Year Built 2000
Approximate Sq. Ft. 2,000

85

"The layout of our home is a perfect balance of roomy spaces for entertaining and cozy places when we want to just curl up with a good book."

Cathy Mullen

Take a few steps into Dennis and Cathy Mullen's 18-room traditional brick home in Pittsford and you're immediately impressed with its high ceilings, large grilled windows, wood-paneled walls, and spectacular walnut center staircase with twin balconies.

"Though the kitchen is our year-round gathering place," Cathy said, "in colder months, we really enjoy the warmth of our family room's two-story stone fireplace."

Ask their daughter what her favorite part of the house is and she'll tell you it's her dance room. "To prepare herself for a future role in a Broadway musical, she spends countless hours practicing there," her mom said.

Like the stately Queen Anne-inspired living room, the home's well-stocked library is warm and welcoming. The latter room, which overlooks the spacious front yard, has a comfy leather couch that's perfect for reading or just enjoying a glass of wine with friends.

Style   Traditional
Year Built   1989
Approximate Sq. Ft. 8,000

87

"After 14 years of renovating, we have the house we've always wanted. It reflects our taste and the way we like to live."

Lori Van Dusen

When Lori and Ron purchased their Victorian-style home in 1990 they were intrigued by its century-old history. They learned it had been a carriage stop in the 1880s, an inn, a single-family farmhouse, and finally a multi-family house just before they bought it.

Back in 1990, it may have been hard for the Boillats to envision what their Pittsford home would look like fifteen years later. Their careful renovation process ensured a seamless integration of the sizeable newer sections with the original rooms of the house. One would be hard pressed to find evidence of the several additions that have made this striking home ideal for 21st-century living.

"Today, our home really flows from one room to the next, far better than it did when we bought it," Lori said. One of her favorite rooms is the large kitchen with its custom cherry cabinets, professional range, granite countertops, and loads of gathering space when entertaining.

Style   Victorian farmhouse
Renovated   1991-2005
Approximate Sq. Ft. 5,600

"Our apartment reflects our love of art,
from celebrated national and local artists.
We find it perfect for entertaining."

Rob Tortorella

Rob said he and his teenage daughter decided to move into The Sagamore on East as soon as it opened. "We wanted to simplify our lives, become city residents, and enjoy the many cultural activities that are nearby," he said. "It was great being the first owners in the building."

When one is inside their spacious East Avenue home, it's hard to believe it's a condo. Each element of their living space is functional, beautiful, and easily accessible, meeting Rob's special mobility needs. The interior designer worked closely with Rob to design an

environment in which almost everything can be controlled remotely, from window shades to a sophisticated entertainment system.

A serious collector of fine art, Rob worked with a local metal artist on several projects throughout his home, including a striking steel archway that separates the living room and entrance foyer.

Style Contemporary
Year Built 2005
Approximate Sq. Ft. 2,250

"This Center holds the pride and promise of a thriving food and wine industry across New York State."

Patrick Brennan
New York State Agriculture Commissioner

One thing is clear as you enter the striking New York Wine & Culinary Center: the wine and food industry in our state is definitely alive and well.

The purpose of the Center, located at the north end of Canandaigua Lake, is to give visitors a taste of what our state has to offer. "Then we expect people to go on to explore the bounty of New York State on their own," executive director Alexa Gifford said.

The building, which opened in June 2006, went from dream to reality in 10 short months. Four founding partners were behind the ambitious project: Constellation Brands, Wegmans,

Rochester Institute of Technology (RIT), and the New York Wine & Grape Foundation.

The handsome exterior combines a number of classic New England architectural cues: gables, buttressed roof soffits, sailcloth clapboard siding with off-white trim, and a wraparound deck. Inside, pegged, timber-frame construction is complemented by rich wood, tiled, and stone surfaces. There is even a private dining room—designed to resemble a winemaker's cellar—and a well-equipped, hands-on kitchen able to host cooking classes for up to 28 students.

Style   Northeast Shingle
Year Built   2006
Approximate Sq. Ft.   20,000

Randall Tagg Photography

93

SAVOR & SAMPLE WHAT MAKES OUR REGION GREAT.

NEW YORK
WINE & CULINARY
CENTER
agriculture · food · wine

Come visit us. Learn how to create your own culinary masterpieces or become a wine connoisseur. Sample great foods and wines, take cooking classes, watch interactive programs, and learn about the vineyards and restaurants that make the 14-county Finger Lakes region a tourist destination like no other.

Located at the northern end of beautiful Canandaigua Lake, the New York Wine & Culinary Center is a stunning 20,000 sq. ft. facility with something for everyone, from wine aficionados to budding chefs.

Come see for yourself all that the gateway to New York State's thriving wine and culinary industries has to offer. You'll be glad you did.

NEW YORK WINE & CULINARY CENTER
800 SOUTH MAIN STREET
CANANDAIGUA, NY 14424 · 585.394.7070
WWW.NYWCC.COM

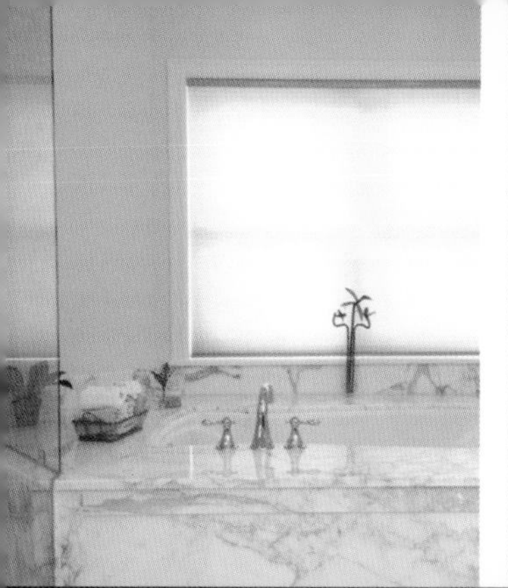
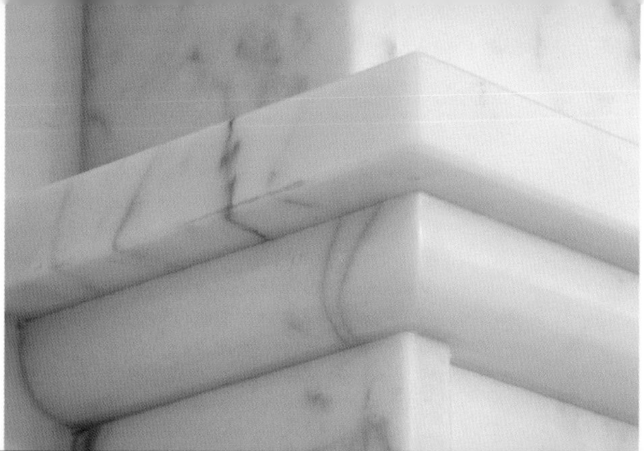

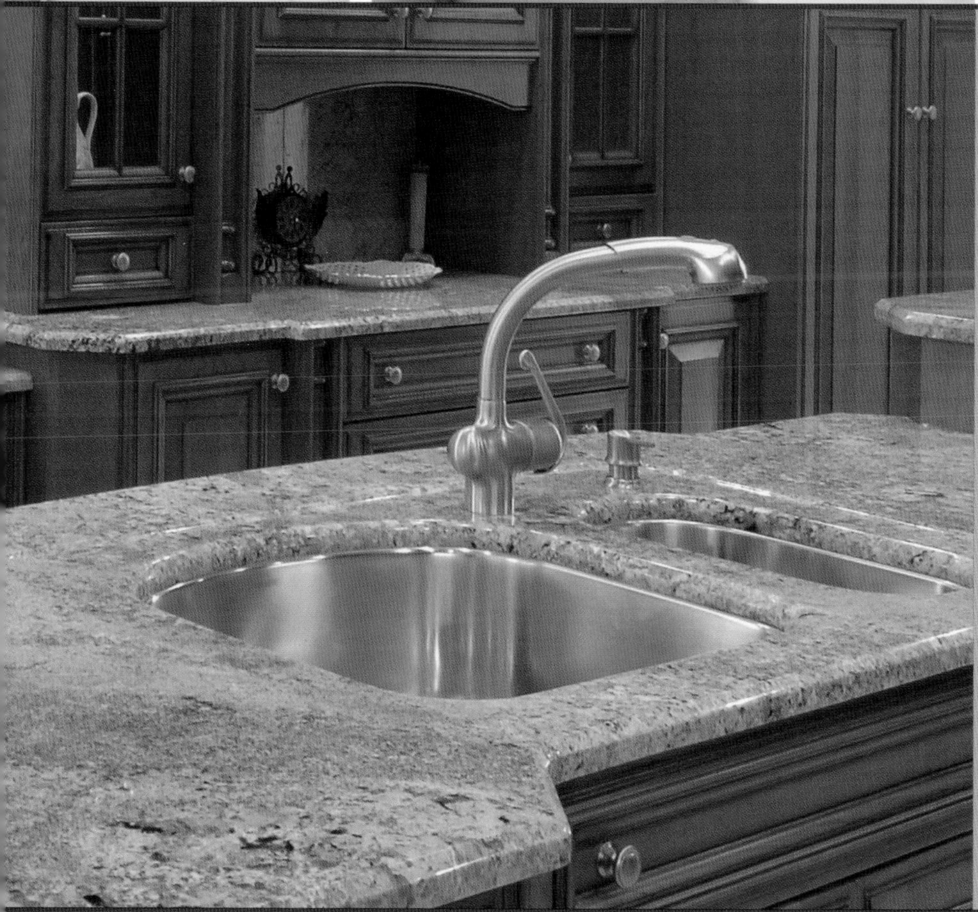

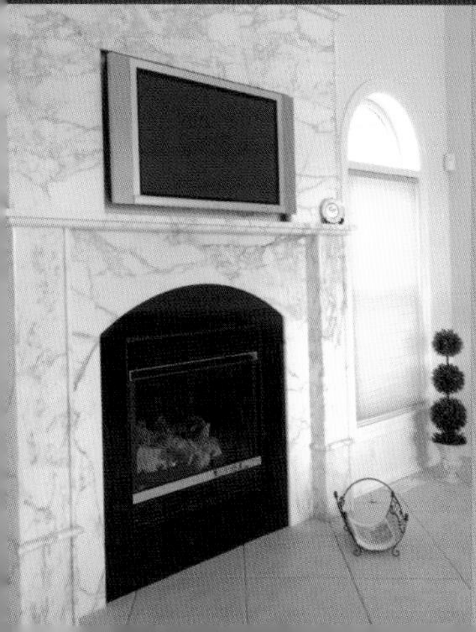

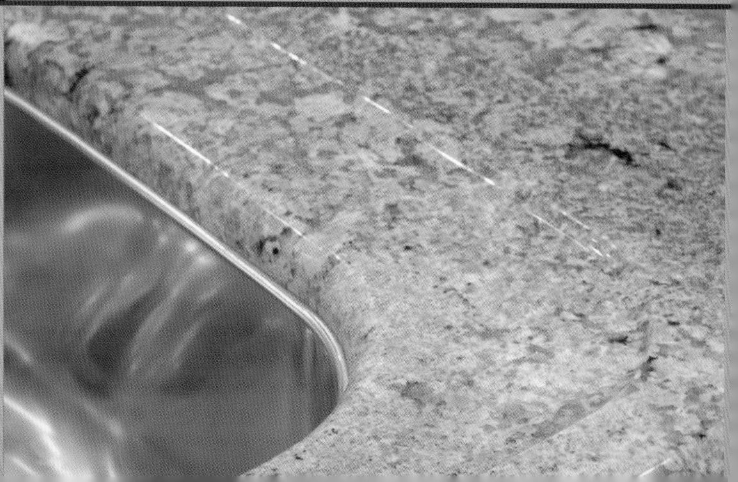

Where great style meets great taste.

Wine, beer and spirits for every occasion

Constellation

SHOPPING EVERYWHERE. For every reason, for every season.

THREE GREAT MALLS, OVER 500 STORES, BOUTIQUES, AND RESTAURANTS.
GREATER ROCHESTER, WE'VE GOT YOU COVERED.

THE **MARKETPLACE** MALL	EASTVIEW A HIGHER FORM *of* SHOPPING	The Mall AT GREECE RIDGE
Hylan Drive and Jefferson Road Henrietta 585.475.0757 www.themarketplacemall.com	Route 96 Victor 585.223.4420 www.eastviewmall.com	Ridge Road West Greece 585.225.0430 www.themallatgreeceridge.com

INDEX